End my Marriage

The Trial of Ana Colon

Written by

Vanessa Concepcion- Limage

Cover illustrated by Mathew Guerrero

copyrights@vanessacon

Only i have rights to this book

This book is inspired by true events. There was a couple in the 17th century, named Denis and Anne Clarke. Both are known for being the first recorded couple divorced in America. (1643). This book, even though fictional, is my version of their story. Hopefully this version gives justice. I guess you shall see.

Content Warnings: Trauma, physical, verbal, intimidating and sexual abuse. Including Animal cruelty, perhaps that could stir up some emotions,etc.

Contents

End my Marriage: The Trial of Ana Colon

This is the story of a woman renowned for her grace and quiet patience—until the life she believed she was building begins to unravel. She marries the man she is certain is her forever, only to uncover secrets from his past that cast long shadows over their marriage. Those revelations change not only how her husband treats her, but how the world around her comes to see her.

Discover the cost of reclaiming dignity once it has been taken, and the courage required to restore a reputation shaped by another's sins. Step inside a tale where the past refuses to stay buried, and the future is uncertain—but not without hope.

Dedications

I dedicate this book to Denis and Anne Clarke, recognized as the first recorded couple to be divorced in America (1643).

I also dedicate this work to my supportive husband, my wonderful children, my sisters, and my father, who listened patiently as I spoke about this story and how deeply it connected me to the past.

Lastly, to my best friend—your encouragement and belief in me gave me the confidence to come as far as I have.

Content Warnings: Trauma, physical, verbal, intimidating and sexual abuse. Including Animal cruelty, perhaps that could stir up some emotions,etc.

Short Prologue

A woman stands at a window, candlelight flickering across her faceShe knows the choice before her... may be the greatest mistake of her life. There is a knock on her door. It's one of the maidens that watch over her children.

"Madam, your children are here to bid you farewell."

As the door opens, the children Elizabeth and William come running towards her.

Elizabeth is 7 years of age and William 3. Tears ran down her face as they hugged her and she dropped to her knees as they embraced her.

Tears fall. She kisses their hair, holding them fiercely.

She whispered in their tiny little ears. "Come what will, I perform this work for thee and for thy sake, my children."

The Maiden responds, "Madam, if I may be so bold. Thou doest this for us all."

End my Marriage

The Trial of Ana Colon

Chapter I

The Beginning of her side of the story

Part 1

It was the end of the month of December, year 1643, in Massachusetts Bay Colony.

The weather had been gently tolerable until the turn of the new year, when winter arrived with sudden force. The cold grew so severe that the windows of the houses filmed over with frozen moisture, trapped by the warmth and breath within. Hands disappeared beneath scarves and thick gloves, and the streets moved at a cautious, hurried pace.

Yet though the cold gnawed at cloaks and stiffened breath into mist, within the Quarter Court of Boston, Massachusetts, a matter of far heavier consequence gathered warmth enough to banish winter from men's thoughts. A trial had been called—Ana Colon v. David Colon—and no frost upon the earth could lessen the gravity of what was to be spoken beneath that roof.

The defendant, David Colon, sat at the left-hand table, his posture held in rigid composure. Opposite him, to the right, the plaintiff, Ana Colon, kept her place, the distance between them small in measure yet vast in meaning.

The charge before the court was plain in wording yet severe in spirit: that David Colon had abandoned his lawful wife and taken himself to another woman, whom he had likewise married.

Thus the case was brought forth upon claims of both desertion and adultery, offenses not only against the bonds of matrimony but against the order by which households stood.

Ana, in her plea to the Quarter Court of Boston, sought more than judgment for herself alone. She asked the magistrates to consider the example set before the community—how such conduct marked not only her honor, but the expectations held within every marriage, and how men might reckon their duties should such actions go unanswered.

"My Lord, must this villainy go unpunished?" After all this while, this is made known to me. After having given myself purely unto him, and being blessed with his Childlings, What will the Mistresses of the parish say of this?" Ana looked around to the people with a concerned look.

"They too would come to question the fidelity and vow of their husbands". She tried to get them to understand what it means to be in this position.

A gentleman did start to his feet and roar, "No woman shall hold us to account!" Have you no shame, to utter such slander?" His name is Jacob Lagoon. known for beating his wife behind closed doors and from time to time visiting the unholy side of town. There are rumors of him giving attention to unholy women out there over nights.

A murmur first stirred along the benches, soft as wind through dry reeds—then swelled at once into clamor. Voices rose sharp and unrestrained; the men called out their agreement in loud approval, while the women answered with indignant breaths, their brows drawn and eyes alight with anger, as though the very air of the chamber had been struck to heat.

"I will have silence in this court!" The judge says out loud and bangs his gavel against the top of his bench table top.

Ana just sat down as tears ran down her face. She felt useless and she knew there were more men than women and her feelings would not matter at this moment.

One of the members of the court looks at the plaintiff and feels a bit saddened by her tears and says out loud "let us take a moment to collect ourselves." The members agree and get up slowly, beginning to exit the court.

Ana rose and made for the exit, each step measured though her composure trembled. Behind her, Mr. Colon watched in silence while she struggled to master the tears threatening to betray her.

She had nearly reached the courtroom door when she felt a stare upon her—hot and pressing, like the sun at the height of summer striking the side of her face. Turning slightly, she saw Mr. Lagoon, the very man who had so rudely broken into her words during the hearing.

Her gaze lingered only a moment. With anger stiffening her posture, she faced the door again and departed with all the swiftness dignity would allow. She would not grant that scoundrel the satisfaction of witnessing her broken, nor leave him thinking her a fool abandoned before the court.

She withdrew to the privy chamber, where the noise of the hall fell to a distant murmur. There she bent over the basin and washed the tears from her cheeks, as though the cool water might cleanse away the humiliation of standing alone before so many judging eyes. Yet though the dampness faded from her skin, the sting within her pride was slower to yield.

She could not fathom how matters had come to such a pass. What cause could drive a man to forsake his wife and child, and cast them aside for the promise of a new life elsewhere? She steadied her hands, set powder lightly upon her face, and turned again toward the courtroom.

Yet before she might cross the threshold, Jacob Lagoon stepped from the passage and drew near. Leaning close, he bent to her ear and spoke in a whisper meant for her alone.

"If he hath turned his back to thee, I may find some small use for another body in my dwelling. For truly, none other would take thee, but my bed will not be so cold for thy lying." Jacob walked away smiling like he had a fortune to actually be with her.

The nearness of him left her with a feeling she could scarcely name—only that she longed for cleansing, as though holy water itself were needed to banish the thought of his touch. A shiver passed over her, and her skin crawled beneath her sleeves.

Yet she gathered herself and entered with her head held high, crossing toward the front of the courtroom with deliberate steps. As she passed the benches, her eyes fell upon a familiar face. There, in the third row, sat Mark—her companion of twenty-five years—watching her with a gentle, reassuring smile.

His presence steadied her at once. Knowing he had come to stand beside her lent strength where moments before there had been none. And at the sight of him, her mind wandered back across the years, to the days when he would arrive by cargo ship to visit her, the harbor wind in his coat and laughter ready upon his lips. Memories rose about her like a tide, warm and unbidden.

Back in the earlier years of boston

Mark's father was a carpenter in the service of the ships that came and went with steady regularity. Often he brought the boy with him, saying a lad must learn early what honest labor looked like in the hands of men.

When the work kept them ashore, they lodged a night or two in a small cottage standing behind the Hockin manor, some four hundred feet from the saloon where his father spent the greater part of his hours. While the elder spoke of timber and fittings among sailors and tradesmen, Mark roamed wherever curiosity led him.

He had always been drawn to what was new, delighting in sights not yet familiar to his young eyes. One afternoon his wandering carried him to the edge of a broad pond. There he stopped, for upon a flat stone sat a girl near his own age, her feet trailing in the water as she sang softly to herself, unaware she had gained an audience.

"Yeah, down by the river

Down by the banks,

of the river ..."

He watched her for a moment, then smiled and spoke, his voice carrying an accent unlike hers, for he had come from the distant town of London.

"What sort of tune is that for a maid of such a tender age?" Ana jumped up startled for a second because she normally was here by herself at that time.

"Pray, sir, is it your purpose to engage in such eavesdropping upon a lady as myself?" She said sarcastically.

"Rest easy, I am not upon some 'worming trade,' only observing the comings and goings. Verily, a fine plot of land this be." He began taking off his boots and she just looked at him confused.

"A fair and curious town, to be sure, but not one to hazard a plunge into such troubled waters." She said as she watched him take off his shirt.

Startled, she colored at once, a faint blush rising to her cheeks.

She turned her head aside as though to grant him the courtesy of privacy—yet curiosity soon betrayed her. She glanced back, then away again, and once more returned her gaze, unable to resist the pull of the unfamiliar boy at the water's edge.

"Verily, I have come to believe these waters be of a sort I know not, for I have been cast about in many interesting currents, and these are not of their number." He smiled and just jumped in as though he has jumped in this pond many times over.

Ana just looked in the water with terror in hopes he would rise back up again safely. A few seconds later he arose back up with seaweed all on top of his head. He said "I concede the point. This is the vilest water I have ever found myself within." They both laughed.

They became closer over time and have been friends ever since no matter how far he was, he would always come back to her land to see her, even when there wasn't work.

A few years after Ana and Mark met

One day when he was older, around 18 years of age, he came back to the dock where she always awaited his arrival.

David Colon got off the same boat as well at this time she had no knowledge of who he was at all.

David walked off the boat with confidence as though he was a king on some land. His head was held high, and he had a well-kept beard. He had a fitting dark blue jacket; a well fitted trouser as well. His trousers had neat legs, his clothes had that classic British feel about them.

Ana could tell he did not do much with his hands because by looking at them from a certain angle he didn't have rough hands at all. His nails were well kept as well and very clean. Ana noticed him quickly as he came before Mark did. He must have noticed her staring when he started walking up towards her way.

"Good morning, fair Mistress, or mayhaps your station is higher? I have a desperate thirst for a draught of ale or wine. Canst thou direct me to a tavern?" He smiled so confidently and somehow made Ana's heart skip a beat.

"It is Mistress." She responded fairly quickly. "It lies but a small distance behind us. Nigh on a mile, mayhap. You shall not fail to find it." Her friend Mark walked up to them while they were talking.Seeming interested in who this gentleman was chatting with his best friend.

David and Ana were both looking at the people headed straight down the way. Ana was pointing towards that way to guide him the right way.

"The gentleman was in search of a public house to wet his whistle." Ana quickly said to Mark before his nosey self could ask.

"Follow the concerned man that alighted from that barque behind us. He goes to cast up his accounts, I warrant you." Mark pointed in that direction and they both laughed as Ana smiled.

"Much obliged, I am much beholden to you,." He says as he walks away. While David strolled towards the man who was told he was losing his liver, he quickly looked back at a second glance at Ana.

He smiled with a hint of flirting and turned his head back to pay attention to his efforts towards the saloon. That is when David and Ana had their first real moment.

Ana smiled as she thought about her friend Mark being there but realized this was no time to smile and this must be taken seriously.

“Be seated, we are about to commence.” The murmur of the room softened, as though the very walls held their breath. One by one, all present composed themselves, their attention fixed upon the bench—upon the judge—and the solemn gentlemen seated to the side, whose watchful eyes would bear witness and, in time, determine her fate.

"Articulate your tale, to the court.” The judge was ready to hear both sides of their stories.

The plaintiff's lawyer, Mr. Huxley gets up and looks around the court and says "Much obliged.To show you Mistress Colon's present troubles. Thou shalt see her past."

"The truest account of these happenings rests in my client's own words; she did suffer these trials, and of this matter, she is the prime witness." The lawyer turned to Ana and gave a quiet, deliberate nod—an unspoken summons. The moment had arrived; it was time for her to rise and give voice to her story.

"Mistress Colon, pray, could you tell me how your union with Mr. Colon came to be?". She nodded and began to explain how the two had met.

"I was acquainted with him some time before we were courting. By chance, he was one of the initial passengers to disembark from the ship."

"Stay thy tongue! You speak now of matters that do not concern this talk." The defendant David got angry because he just thought it would be over quickly but it's not as easy as he imagined.

"Compose yourself, good sir and you shall discover, if you grant my client a moment to tell her tale." The lawyer says to defend his client.

The Lawyer knew Ana's story was his main evidence and needed the court to hear certain details that would get him where he wanted the case to go.

He remained standing, his expression hard with restrained anger, eyes fixed on his attorney as if awaiting a shield that never came. Instead, the lawyer leaned close and murmured something only he could hear.

Mr. Colon's jaw tightened; a flicker of irritation crossed his face before he lowered himself back into his seat, composed but simmering.

Across the room, Ana continued, her voice steady as she began to recount how they first met.

"The meeting at the dock lay already some days past when my father took himself to a shadowed corner of a Boston tavern, being once more greatly elevated by drink.

I was there present to fetch him away, for the man can no longer bear his liquor with the same vigour he possessed in his younger years."

"I went to look after my father's welfare; I walked unto him and took my place at his side."

3 years back at the saloon where Ana's

father was drinking

"Father, you look quite fatigued; a small lie-down might do you good." Ana says to her father to get him to believe he is ready for sleep. It always seems to help when trying to get him home. Ana had heels about 2 inches high and often had lace frills around the top line with lace rosettes upon her chest line.

She had cream colored skin with dark hazel eyes and dark curly hair pinned up with a black hair pin. With the heels she was 5.6' but when she stands on the ground she is 5' 3. She was known for her beauty and how she was a woman who says what's on her mind.

"Nay, child, slumber not yet, for we shall not find peace in sleep alone. Come, hear a lesson from the Lord, my little Annie." That had been his nickname for her since she was young. He smiled, then took another gulp of ale. A bit missed his mouth and spilled onto his shirt.

"And how might you possess the strength for the morrow, if you do not grant your body rest?" Ana realized her father was getting up.

As she tries to keep him aware of his surroundings, her father starts singing. Swinging his jug from side to side:

"Will spend what he gets,

And drinke more then he eates,

That never meanes to vary

From good fellowship free,"

She took the drink from his hand and set it on the bar as they passed, then tried to guide him toward the saloon's exit.

He was stronger than she was, and she struggled to keep him upright as they walked.

Just before they reached the door, his weight sagged heavily against her and her grip began to slip. As he started to fall from her hold, David appeared beside them and caught her father on his left side.

He lifted the man's arm over his shoulder and steadied him, all while her father continued singing — David joining in with him as they made their way out.

"If thou such a one be..
Ile drinke to thee kinde Harry."

As they make it out of the saloon, they both stop for a second. He looks at Ana and says "Miss, which way do we proceed?"

She looks at him confused. "Pardon me, Mr umm.?" She forgets his name.

"My appellation is David, I am not one for idle words, As I have heretofore been of service to thy father, to lend him my body as a cushion." He smiles as Ana's dad's head tends to go sideways as he is falling asleep.

"David, I shall attend to this forthwith, you are no servant bound by a contract" She tries to grab her dad from him, so she can continue on to their home.

As she grabs him, he starts to snore and mumbles nonsense in his sleep. "Landlord, another mug of ale, if you please" drool slides down her father's mouth.

"Dust thou take assurance of it Ana? I am heading that way anyway." Ana was puzzled; he remembered her name.

"I pray, point the way to that." She looked at him for an answer. Her dad was slowly falling out of her arms.

"It is not for me to say, but for thee to confess." He just smiled.

She nodded to the right, letting him help her this one time, because she did not have the strength to drag her father this time around. She felt like she could use a small break so she did not fight the gentleman. He smiled and grabbed her father more for a better grip as they walked.

They walked past the other small shops and around the lake area where she and Henry met. They finally made it to the cottage. David did not let go of Ana's father yet his body was getting weary.

"I beg of thee, that I might but see him to his bed." "I will not trouble you." He looked at her seriously.

"We are well. We fare well, I thank ye for making the journey. God willing, I shall one day be able to return the favor." She goes to take her father inside, and he stares and waits for her to be within her door.

"Make no matter of it. May he receive the rest that his body requires." He started to walk away.

"And you, sir." She remembered but was just messing with him.

"No, 'tis not, Sir. Only David." He smiled.

A few hours later, David returned to her home. He knocked lightly, not wanting to be harsh at such a late hour.

Ana came to the door and opened it, surprised to see him again for the second time that day. She wore a slip, her right thumb and forefinger

pressed close together in a small, nervous gesture..

"It is with a grateful and humble spirit that I again welcome you, for I did not expect to be so favored by Providence twice on this same night."

"I must pray to your honor's indulgence for disturbing you from your rest."

"I came only to inquire of thy father's health". He seemed really concerned.

"Well, if there is poison, he has drunk it more than enough times, his body is now the poison itself.One may say he is immune" They both laughed very lightly.

"That's good to know." He smiled and somehow got Ana's attention.

"I am actually cooking supper as we speak. May you want something warm to fill your body on such a night?" She knew she had to be kind. He was kind and funny. How many people can act with such matters around this town?

"Well, that would be dandy. Because I have not filled my body with anything cold or hot since morning time." Ana opened the door more letting David enter their home.

While waiting near the door he overheard Ana's father say out loud.
"Make haste, my son, and partake of the victuals laid upon the board.

My daughter doth speak of the great kindness thou hast shown her, and one good turn deserveth another. Sit thee down, for supper is made ready."David moved deeper into the home.

Ana's father, Joseph, wore a long beard streaked black and gray. The hair had grown coarse with age, yet he still carried himself with a certain strength. He handled his horses with the ease of a whisperer and could outdrink nearly any man at the saloon.

Joseph sat at the refectory's wooden table, surrounded by four carved curule chairs.

David remained standing beside one of them, waiting for Ana to take her seat as a sign of respect. He had been taught that the head of the table should sit before any guest.

Yet in this moment, Ana seemed to hold that place of honor, her father's condition shifting the balance of the room. One could still see that he remained present within himself—but not entirely. "You may be seated, David," Ana said as her hand jested towards the seat.

"I am much obliged, madam." As he sat Ana questioned David "Madam?" "I expect that you mean, My years are not so many as to merit that title." She smiled and David did so as well.

Her father, Henry, looked at David and said, "Aye, I know thy face well. We have been much about the same spaces.What caused you to arrive upon this land? Are you a merchant or a tradesman?" Henry seemed very focused on getting to know David for some reason.

"I have been in service for some time now, but I am here on thy land. I might stay here for a bit longer."

"I am in sore need of a hand with my husbandry. If you are inclined to that which is different and Thou appear'st a stout and able lad, well-suited to the labor at hand. Lend me a hand with this, will you?"

"I would humbly be grateful for the opportunity, yet I have no certain knowledge of how husbandry is practiced hereabouts." David answered back.

"My daughter and I shall show thee, and thy needs shall be met" Ana looked at her father surprised.

"It would seem he has determined our course for us both. I expect thy presence here with the first light of the morrow, without delay." Ana said professionally.

David nodded and smiled. "Yes mistress, I mean Ms. Ana."

Part 2

At the present time in the courtroom

"Bemoidered in my understanding. This bears no purpose upon our current station. Let us not recall former tales." Mr. David said to his lawyer but out loud for the court to hear.

"David, you must hear the history to know why the madam is thus distressed and here on this day." The plaintiff's lawyer stated back.

"I did bear witness to why we must again open the ancient sores." He seemed furious this time. David was not ready for those in this courtroom to hear about his past.

"David, let them proceed." The judge said firmly.

"I am much obliged to you, sir." Ana's lawyer said.

"Pray, continue, Anna." The lawyer stated to his client nodded and she continued.

3 years back at the farm

Ana is out on the farm feeding her four horses. She hears a "Ow!" sound, and she walks over to the pig side of the farm.

Knowing who it would be making that noise, she smiled.

As we entered the pigpen, Ana noticed David sitting in the mud bath of the pigs looking relinquished. As though there was a fight that he surely lost.

"Master David, thou dost seem to be sorely tried by these afflictions. or wanting to bathe with the hogling. Which one am I correct about?" She smiled and tried not to laugh out loud.

"I am definitely not resting; nay, these hoglings do well know how to o'ercome a gentleman, despite their want of stature." Ana reaches out to help David get out of the mud. He smiles and gets out safely.
"Well, some of these young swine are passing finicky, I warrant ye. As this one here doth prove." Ana pointed at the big pig at the end of the mud pond lying against the fence.

"She will do naught unless you rouse her with a carrot or an ear of Indian corn. She doth much enjoy chewing upon the cob part, for I do think it serves to help her teeth." Milly turns, looks at Ana and closes her eyes again.

"I would have been if I were apprised of the rules sooner." He said as his eyebrows raised higher than normal.

"And where, pray, is the merriment in that?" She laughed and walked off to the pig pen area.

"Let's get you some other garment, for the horse doth smell thee out. Thou art but inviting a kicking." They both laughed, and David followed her into the cabin.

As he received his new clothes and was back being all cleaned up, he went out of the room into the kitchen area.

Where Anna was making lunch. She was cutting the loaf into smaller pieces. David looked at her and said, "May I be of service?"

"Marry, what a conceit is here! I ne'er before had a gentleman seek to lay a hand to his victuals in such a fashion, then to stuff his maw." Ana smiles, knowing this will annoy him. "Marry, ha I am not of that common sort."

"I have capacities that my mother imparted to me before she departed this life." He comes closer to her and grabs the bread slowly out of her hand as he looks into her eyes in a flirting way.

She gives him the bread cutter and proceeds to the other side of the table to see his skills.

As he slowly cuts the bread so easily, she can't help but notice his forearm muscles budge a bit through his garment. She almost bit her lip, but got out of the trance once her dad came strolling in.

"Alack, I am famished. They did not use me civilly today." He looked at David with the bread and was confused. "When did we suffer our guests to prepare their own victuals?"

"Father, he is no longer a stranger once he tumbles into the mire (or fen), and he offers a hand."

Her father gave him a sleek look. "Is it so?"

"Aye, sir, I warrant you all is well. My mother did afford me a glimpse of this, and I simply desired to display it unto the mistress of the house." David took a quick glance at her and continued cutting.

"Well, isn't that a civil part of him, Ana?" He looked at her as though he knew David was trying to impress her.

"Indeed, he is, father. Now let us sit and partake of our meal." David stops slicing the bread and washes his hands and sits down with Ana and her father.

"This hath a most savoury scent." David says, referring to the food at the table.

"If thou dost relish that same odour every morn,If thou wouldst, in truth, hold it in great affection daily, didst thou but as a honer opt to make a suit for my daughter." Ana's father smiled at David.

"Father, I am not for any man's suit!" Ana got so angry at her dad her face turned red. In her mind she should have a say about what or who she wants to be with, even if this were the rule. Parents choose who their kids should marry. Which Ana does not agree with.

They sit and enjoy their food."I trust this loaf is cut to thy liking.I know thou mayst not desire to be woo'd, yet I pray thee, take no offence that thou shouldst be well fed."He smiled at her.
She smiled without looking at him and spoke.

"In sooth, I must confess, 'tis a most agreeable thing to prepare one's victuals not in solitude."

"Pray, what concern hath this matter with the affairs of this present day?" Mr. Colon says out loud in court.

"Good sir, pray allow the lady to tell her tale" The judge said, almost annoyed with David at this point.

"I just think this is hysterical." He laughed but you can see the fear he had.

"I know you did hold yourself a gentleman then." Mrs. Colon says and looks at him with a straight face ready to tell her side. He just stood quiet and put his head down.

"Continue , Mrs Colon," the lawyer said to her.

"That was the day my heart was smitten by him. Well, I deemed he was. We were married a few weeks hence."

"My father was happy, and so was I "She smiled for a second then became sad again.

"If you were happy, wherefore are we here today?" The defendant's lawyer asked.

"For that I was deceiv'd, and he became so alter'd after we were link'd in marriage." Mrs. Colon answered.

"How did he change?" quoth her counsel.

"Verily, after we were wed, I would sometimes find him at the tavern, neglecting the care of the farm." Ana continued.

"What miserie attended to thirst? Am I not to have a quaff?" David looked around at the men to agree and they nodded with full agreement .

"Not when thou art put to labour in the field." She looked at the judge and said. "He would carouse for hours. I would have to hale him out of the tavern just to get him home."

"Is it not the wont of most fellows to keep one another's company? Be it on matters of trade or simply taking leisure for male fellowship?" The defendant's lawyer asked out loud.

"Marry, under normal consideration 'twould be well, but we were so o'erwrought with labour on the farm, and my sire was taken ill, and I could not manage it all myself." She became sad because her father died a few months ago.

"Is this true, Mr. Colon?" The judge looked at David Suspicious.

"But it was a dark season for me. I am better now, and my blood is pure.That was my weakness, and since I have sought it out, my Lord, I am a better man" He hoped for sympathy from the whole court.

He did get better, but it just happened after Ana's father died, but he did just go down a dark hole before he became who he is today. Just went down

"I am glad to hear this." He then picks up his Gavel and says " Let's take a few moments to quench our thirst. We will be back soon." He hit his gavel on the podium. Everyone started to make their way out of the courtroom.

The people viewing the case left the room first. Then the defendant and his lawyer were next.

As the judge and his group of judicial clerks (who help him throughout the cases) are excited towards the back to exit. And lastly, the plaintiff and her lawyers have time to exit. By the time she exited the courtroom, her old friend was waiting just outside the door near the left side of the bench.

"Well, hello old friend," he says as he smiles at her.

"Thou canst not fathom the passions that arise within me upon the sight of thy most handsome countenance." She kissed him on the left cheek.

"Well I wot that the number of thy companions shall be but slender, for he hath many who stand steadfastly at his side." He took a quick glance at the crowd that was around him as if he was king of the land.

All they saw was many gentlemen going to him shaking his hand and complimenting him in one way or another.

While their wives stood behind them like a dog waiting for their master to be done talking.

Chapter II

In the chambers

As the gentleman begins to sit around the room and the judge sits at his desk, they begin to discuss the case.

"Your Honour, I am much perplexed as to why this matter yet endureth; for all do know that no wedded pair may be sunder'd save by death itself."

In that time it was unheard of a separation unless a husband or wife lost their lives, and then they were appointed a new person to live

out the rest of their lives within a week of mourning.

"There was great ado made of this matter by the folk of D.C., and none of it was of my own choosing. Yet, in sooth, I take some pleasure in the spectacle." The judge and clerks laughed all but one.

"I deem not this a mere spectacle, but rather a shameful affront unto men in all places; and methinks we ought to take earnest heed of it." Eric, one of the clerks, stared at him for a second, then looked at the judge. The judge began to laugh, and then the clerks laughed after him.

"We shall trouble ourselves over naught, boy. This is my own court, and I counsel thee to govern thy tongue—both within these walls and without." The judge's face turned bitter.

"None do dare to call the Judge into question." One of the clerks said out loud. All the clerks agreed by nodding and laughing.

"I throw this matter shall conclude as swiftly as ever it began." The judge said really confidently.

Aye, I am of the same mind. For, as hath been told, whomsoever he was said to have wed where he came to her is departed from this mortal world. Thus, ponder well the scant proof that lieth before us." He said proudly.

"Yet again I do inquire: wherefore dost thou pursue this case at all?" The 1st clerk says defending his first question.

"Ye men do behold this matter amiss. Consider it thus: if certain women know of this fellow and of his deeds, think ye not that our own wives shall begin to question our faith and constancy?" He was starting to make sense of what he was saying, and the clerks started to have worried looks on their faces.

"How meanest thou, that they should question us? No woman ought to question so much as a single damn'd thing!" The judge bangs his fist on his desk. He couldn't believe as a judge that he had to go through this just for some woman who was not worth his time.

"We may but wish it were so, yet the courses of our lives do differ greatly from thine own." He responded.
"My wife is ever railing at me; I can brook no more of her ceaseless chiding o'er matters of no account. I have no stomach for further

clamor." A clerk talked about his wife and started to sound stressed.

Thou seest, Your Honour; we are not all endued with such felicity." Eric looked at the judge. "All that I would say is this: let us bear ourselves with some measure of solemnity, that we may return unto our wives and avouch that we did strive with all our might."

The group were all in agreement as they nodded their heads.
They all began to drink before they decided to help get back to court.

About fifteen minutes later, they began to head back into the courtroom. But before the clerks and the judge entered the courtroom, one clerk whispered in Eric's ear. "I would not have my wife learn aught of my harlot; I dare not forfeit her."

"Well, let us hope she shall not put forth such questions." Eric smiled and walked away with the rest of the men.

As they all sit down and get ready for the defendant to talk to Mrs. Colon looks his way, and then he looks back and winks at her. She quickly turns away to look at the judge.

The judge says to the defendant's lawyer, "Is thy client prepared to speak his peace?"

"Aye, he is, Your Honour." The defendant's lawyer named Bill answered.

"Then thou mayest proceed, Mr. Colon." he said, as he nodded.

"I thank thee, Your Honour." Mr. Colon said.

"Now, though it may sound as some tale of love, it was in truth naught of the kind." Mr. Colon says as he smiles at her.

"To utter falsehoods in this court tendeth unto perjury, Mr. Colon." the Plaintiff's lawyer stated for the court to hear.

"I did no such deed. I was but her servant, never her husband. She would have naught of me save that I labour from dawn till dusk." David seemed angry As telling his side.

"When she granted me lodging within her house, little did I know I should become her slave." He shakes his head.

"Her slave, sayest thou? Is that not somewhat overbold, Mr. Colon?" The judge mentioned.

"Nay, Your Honour. I rose each morn to a long bill of tasks, even as I lay me down each night sore spent from the day's toil. Thus, aye, I do take a draught now and again, for such small liberty is mine to claim." He felt the men understood because many of them in the courtroom nodded.

"Didst thou deem thyself to have done all within thy power to grant Master Colon contentment?" The Defendant's lawyer asked.

"In sooth, I most assuredly did!" As he said that you hear a huff come from Ana herself.

"I did, and claim no less." He said to Ana with anger.

"I spoke not; yet had I spoken, I would have said this: thou mayest indeed have done thy part at the first, but as time wore on, thou wert but half a laborer and but half a living soul within our marriage." She kept her head high as though she had nothing to hide.

"Compose thyself, Mistress Colon, and let the man speak his peace." The judge said to Ana.

"And what if he should deal falsely with this court, Your Honour?" She questions his side of the story.

"That lieth with us to determine, Mistress Colon." He said very seriously.

She looked a bit angry but respected the court enough to know when it's time to be silent.

"I thank thee, Your Honour." David Colon said to the judge.

"Thou mayest proceed."He responded.

"After the day we were wed, she straightway grew more demanding."

Back at the barn

David was eating at the table eating his cornmeal mush and milk. As Ana walks up to him.

"The kine are yet unfed, and the hour is already past eight, whilst thou thyself hast broken thy fast. I counsel thee, therefore, to tend them forthwith, lest thou have no milk for thy cup upon the morrow." She then walks away going to the room to discuss something with her father.

David did not like her tone but there was work that needed to be done. He only finished half of his breakfast and headed out to the barn. Ana re-entered the dining area and noticed the beaker and bowl on the table left behind by David.

She was furious she hated such things left behind especially when she spent the night cleaning to make sure it was spotless. Her mother before she passed used to say to her when she was younger a woman's job is to keep the home spotless. "It maketh us of some importance." She used to say. That stood in her mind for so long. So when she sees things like this it makes her feel less important. Which makes her upset.

She took the items and placed them to wash but before she did so she walked over to where David was at the barn and let him know how upset she was.

"I have espied yet another foul disorder thou hast left for me to mend,David." Her face turned red as a tomato. She was tired of cleaning up after him and she had enough.

"Well,I am right glad thou hast made everything so clean." He smiled while focusing on putting hay down for the horses.

"I am thy wife, not thy slave. See that thou pickest up after thyself." She walked away.

Present Time in the courtroom

"Didst thou hear how she spoke unto me? and in public, no less! What if some passer-by had overheard?" He stood up and looked around the room to face the other men so they would feel his anger and disrespect.

In that very moment, a loud laugh broke from Ana herself. The sound echoed through the room, and David's expression darkened as anger began to rise within him.

"What mirth findest thou here? Thou art a most discourteous and choleric woman!" He banged his fist against the desk.

"I find it passing strange that thou takest such jest in the barn being set without, as though all the world might hear us. Yet it was but we two and the horses. Unless some horse hath suddenly been granted a tongue fit for human converse, no mortal ear hath heard a whit."

"Have a care to thy manners, Mrs. Colon." The judge said. He was not a man who would tolerate a woman speaking in such a manner before men—unless she wore a crown.

"Thou seest, Your Honour; she is ever too hasty to speak in such a manner." The men began murmuring among themselves, their voices low and tense, as their eyes fixed upon Mrs. Colon with visible displeasure.

"My client doth offer her apologies, Your Honour. She spoke the truth: though he feared their words might be overheard, naught but the beasts were present to hearken unto them." Ana Lawyers says

"Tis not her time to speak, and hereafter she shall await her turn." The judge responded.
"Of course, Your Honour." Ana responds back.

"As my client hath afore declared, he was sorely afflicted by his wife's harsh usage. Surely this must weigh for something." The plaintiff's lawyer to the judge and the courtroom.

"I do object, Your Honour! He doth falsely charge my client with grave matters upon no proof. 'Tis sheer defamation!" Her lawyer felt he was doing justice stating that but the court just looked at him annoyed if anything.

"Nay, 'tis slander he casteth, for he striketh at her former conduct and even at that which thou seest before thee now. Your Honour, I pray thee, permit my client to finish the telling of his tale."

"He may." The judge nodded.

Both attorneys resumed their seats as the plaintiff began presenting his account.

Chapter *III*

His side of the story

"As men, we are owed our due respect, yet my so-called wife had none for me. She would drag me forth from taverns as though she were my Mother. Once, being in a fine humour after a day's labour, I went to take a draught. But she came, to spoil the gladness of my evening, smiling upon the very fellow that served my drink."

A few years ago at the saloon where David was enjoying his Ale.

David was drinking his 3rd cup of Ale, laughing it up with the other men there.

When he was there, he spent most of his time with two other men who, in his view, understood the burden of hard labor—and the supposed trials of dealing with women.

One of them was Jacob Lagoon, a man in his early thirties who appeared far older, as though the years had not been kind. The crown of his head was nearly bare, with what little hair remained gathered mostly along the lower back portion. He wore it pulled into a small ponytail streaked with black and gray.

He had a stomach that a pregnant woman should have but instead of storing a fetus he stored his Ale and food in it instead.

David often kept him company because he would buy his ale for him. Jacob disliked drinking alone, so whoever happened to be by his side at the time knew he would likely buy a round—or several. He was known for inheriting money from his father, and he treated people accordingly.

He was a European man who showed little regard for women, though he himself was married. His wife was rarely seen in public. Whispers among the women suggested her absence was no coincidence—that he had beaten her so severely at times that she dared not show her face.

The other man in their company was Raphael Bazel, the youngest of the three at just twenty years of age.

He regarded the older men with a misplaced admiration, almost as though they were uncles guiding him into manhood. Raphael's father had died when he was fifteen. His mother claimed he passed quietly in his sleep, yet rumors from the tavern told a darker tale—that he had been heavily intoxicated, fallen, struck his head, and bled to death.

Now he looks to the men at the tavern to shape him, believing he can trust them more than his own mother.

He was a light-skinned youth with hazel eyes and thin, narrow arms that betrayed his age more than his pride would allow.

Despite his slight frame and lack of muscle, he carried himself with the conviction that he was every bit as strong—and every bit as much a man—as the others who gathered at the saloon.

"Thou must drink, boy; it shall make thee a man, even as the rest of us."Jacob said to Raphael. Jacob already drank three cups of Ale and was tipping sideways off the chair.

"Methinks he needeth more than ale to put any manner of muscle upon that frame. He must eat well and labour sturdily."

"Perchance I should hale him to the farm and show him what true toil may work in a man." David says as they both laugh and Rapheal falls closer to the ground.

"Work? Nay, that is not the way of it. 'Tis silver that maketh a man, even though he bears no muscle upon him. Ha ha!" he laughed out loud while grabbing his stomach showing his lack of muscles he has.

As all the gentlemen laughed together, Ana entered the Saloon. Realizing that Rapheal is almost at the floor at this time she heads to him and props him back onto the chair correctly.

"Mayhap ye should seek companions of thine own years to play the drunken fools ye are, rather than prey upon young souls who might yet become something of worth in this life." She took a piece of bread from the bar and carried it to Raphael, urging him to eat so that he might begin to sober up.

Jacob watched Ana with narrowed eyes, his expression hardening, as though her simple act of kindness were some grave offense.

"Why wouldst thou suffer thy wife to serve men that are not thyself?" She turned red and he turned red and Jacob was in shock to hear a woman speak up that way. While Poor Rapheal once again was falling towards the ground.

"Pardon me? *Permit* me? I am the mistress of my own person; no man shall so command me as though I possessed no mind of my own."

Ana began to become very angry.

David glanced at Ana, then shifted his gaze toward Jacob, a flicker of embarrassment crossing his face before he spoke to her. "I beg thy pardon? 'Let me,' sayest thou?

Back in court room in present time

"Wherefore wouldst thou suffer thy wife to minister unto men other than thyself?" The lawyer looked at the judge then turned and looked around to the crowd to see if they were listening.

"I was present, Your Honour. She bore herself with the most discourteous speech. Verily, she deserveth to be taken to task and taught a proper lesson."He had the crowd of men yelling and agreeing.

"Compose yourselves. We shall resume this matter come morning." the judge bangs his gavel on the podium he stood.

"Let us bring this matter to its end forthwith!" David yells at the judge.

The judge looks at him surprised then angry. "Thou hadst best bring thy client to order, else he shall lie this night in the cellar."

"I beg thy pardon, Your Honour; his passions o'ercame him. He was eager to see this matter brought to its end." The lawyer took his client and guided him outside the doors of the courtroom before he talked again.

"What aileth thee? Wouldst thou have the court set thee in irons?" The lawyer is speaking with David.

"This passeth all reason! This woman is a wicked creature who useth men as she doths her horses, and yet *I* am made the villain?" He walks away from his lawyer to exit the building. The lawyer just stood there in disbelief.

Ana walks out of the courtroom last, and she is discussing what's next for tomorrow with her lawyer.

"Only continue as thou hast begun. Let not Master Colon draw thee from thy proper bearing, and all shall be well with thee."He gives her some paperwork to look over for tomorrow's questions.

"Well, I shall do mine utmost, yet his sour tongue may render it somewhat hard to disregard." She smiled.

"He bringeth this ill favor upon himself. Thy charge is to sit you back and behold him dig his own grave and mar his own good name."

"Yea, sir. It shall be done." She smiled, waved and started walking towards the exit. She was smiling knowing she thought she was finally seeing the true him.

As she walked outside saw a bunch of women outside surrounding Jacob. He is smiling and laughing and he is feeling like a king.

You could tell it was his unholy women and as always his wife was nowhere to be found.

As Ana walked past them, they became awfully quiet. Then Ana hears one of the women scream out. "She deserveth no husband; a barn is all the lodging meat for her!" another screamed out.

"She deserveth not a husband; she deserveth a barn!" They all laughed and Ana just put her head down and kept going.

She knew that was not a fight that would go well. Those women have no souls and care in the world. It would end badly for her.

She remembered one day walking to get some dough, for bread for dinner and she saw a bunch of those unholy women, around 10 of them, in an alley yelling and hitting one of their own for taking money from their rooms.

They were not 100% sure it was her but because she was the newest and youngest one it made sense that the blame went to her instead of one of them.

After that day she could not get one man to go to her room or pay her no mind. Eventually she was seen hanging by a tree with a sign on her body with the words (thief) on it.

These women will do anything for money even go after their own.

Ana Finally made it home after her long walk from court. David had the carriage and refused to give her anymore things that belonged to him that he used to do for her.

A few days before the first day of court David came into the room he came in so angry. Ana was sitting down sowing a button bacon on one of the shirts of his that came off days before after riding the horses into town.

"Thou darest to hale me into the courts! Thou darest to bring shame upon me and my kin, all for thy petty jealousy!" He threw court papers at her and started pacing back and forth in the room.

"Jealousy, sayest thou? Ha! As for shame, it is thou who shouldst be abashed—who could forsake wife and children and cast them off as though they had never drawn breath!"

She got up to show she was just as angry as he was and she would not back down.
"How do I know that thou wilt not serve me in like manner? I refuse to become thy next hapless victim!" He looks at her and turns red and next thing she knows he swung his hand across her face making her fall back to her bed.
She was in shock and a bit scared. He has never struck her before. She did not recognize this person who yelled at her like that and abused her in any way.

"Behold what thou hast driven me to!" He just looked at her as though she was a child who needed to be punished.

"How darest thou!" She cried and held her face. That slap hurt more than she thought it would.

"How dare I, sayest thou? Until thou dost release us from this mad proceeding, I shall not use thee as I did aforetime. The love and regard once thine shall be withheld. Thou shalt yield and stand down!" David just walked out the room leaving her in pain and confusion.

It took days before she went back and forth on the decision whether to go through this.

He took away her servants and then next took away her rides to certain places and one happened to be to the courtroom. She began to become angry. She decided after all she will go through it and no matter what he took away she would not let him get the best of her.

How could he even think it was okay to even leave his first wife? Unless he was in some sought of danger Ana could not see how one would leave the one he loved and bore children with.

The only reason she found out was because she was once waiting by the shore for her friend to arrive as always he would come down twice a month and this was the second time of the month.

Four weeks before the court date

Ana waited 20 minutes or so as the ship was being unloaded from men on the boat.

As she waited, a young man—no more than five feet seven—dropped a crate upon a stack of boxes already piled high.

The sound drew her attention, and he looked directly at Ana.

He was light-skinned, with striking orange hair the color of a ripe tangerine, making him impossible to overlook as he walked straight toward her, as though he had known her once before.

"Good madam, I crave pardon for the intrusion, yet I had hoped thou mightest direct me to some house where folk gather to quench their thirst," he said with a warm smile.

Both his manner and his smile stirred something familiar within her, though she could not at once place why.

"Thou must needs be new to this place, sir; for many a man from thy ship knoweth well the path thereto."

The sun's shine was in the gentleman's eye so he took his left palm and tried to cover his eyes from the sun as he spoke to Ana.

"There were naught there but a host of drunkards, and many at that. Pray, give me his name, that I may perchance guide thee unto the right man." she smiled, wanting to help the young man who obviously had a plan and why not make it easier for him since he came so far from she can only assume Ireland.

His eyes and hair are very unique and not many people have such features. It could have been a very easy guess.

"His name is David Colon. Doth that name sound familiar unto thee, or hast thou any inkling who such a man might be?" The young man just looked at her waiting for an answer.

Ana was in shock out of all names that it would be her husband's name. She wondered maybe someone in his family was ill or something may have been wrong. She didn't know much of his family or his past. He always said that to her.

"The past is of no great consequence, for the present is all in all." She didn't pursue any more than that means maybe some stories are not meant to be told and Ana must admit that she loved the mystery of him.

"Well, sir, it doth come to my notice that I may know this man right well." She responded. "May I inquire thy name, youngling? And what business thou hast with this man?" She just looked at him curiously.

"Aye, good madam, and I crave thy pardon.

My name is Nathaniel Colon." Nathaniel took out his hand to wait for her hand and he was taught as a young boy must always introduce himself and kiss the woman's hand when there is an introduction.

She looked at him, smiled then gave him her left hand to kiss. She was not used to this introduction but well along with it.She thought where he was from had to do a lot from his well behaved manners.

"'Tis a pleasure to make thy acquaintance, Nathaniel." She smiled.

"The honour is wholly mine, fair lady. Little did I know I should be so fortunate as to meet such a comely woman, who moreover is acquainted with the very man I seek."

As they were talking, Henry started to make his way towards Ana. He noticed how friendly this young gentleman was towards his best friend. And being that she was wedded he felt protected over her. As he reaches by them he quickly states.

"This is no tree for thee to bark upon, sir; for this tree is already claimed." He stands beside her and smiles as though he solved a problem that was not his to solve.

"Henry, didst thou but now likened it unto a tree?" Ana just looked at Henry with confusion.

"Not exactly." He smiled and took a glance at Nathaniel.

"Not precisely so; yet thou didst liken thyself unto a tree already claimed, therefore it doth seem so to me." she elbowed him discreetly. "Well, notwithstanding this tree—aye, this lady—she is already plighted unto another." He said to Nathaniel as he laughed a bit.

"Well, I do vow unto thee, despite her comeliness, I am come hither for no other purpose than to seek a certain man." He smiled at Nathaniel.

"Well, that is my special talent. I am Henry; glad am I to make thy acquaintance. Yet, I perceive I have not asked thee thy name…"He pulls out his hand for a shake.

"Nathaniel. 'Tis a pleasure to make thy acquaintance." They shook hands.

"He has come hither to seek a particular man, Henry." Ana said as letting him know he was not here for him.

"And who might this fortunate fellow be? Pray, may I inquire?" Henry smiles at him.

"Well, as I was but telling thy goodwife…"Henry giggles at what Nathaniel just said.

"Wife? Ha! Ana is no wife of mine."
Ana looks at him and elbows him one more time.
"Ouch, that one hurt." Henry says while touching the part of his rib that was elbowed.
"Thou shouldst count thyself most fortunate." she laughed

"I crave pardon for his foolish prating. Pray, continue with what thou wast saying." Ana says in return.

"Well, Henry, this was the point at which we were interrupted," she said, speaking of a certain man reputed to be found in a saloon in those parts. She confessed she knew the fellow well.

"Most curious. And who, pray, is this man whom my good friend's lady knoweth so well?"

She just looks at Henry, getting ready to see his facial response, then says, "David." She looks at Nathaniel smiling, still a bit confused who this gentleman was.

"David who?" Henry was unaware of what was going on. Trying to look at them both like, what is he missing?

"My David." Ana said with a straight face.

"Why should he desire thee, David?" quoth Henry. "He is not such a comely man." Henry giggled a bit but Ana was not laughing nor was Nathaniel.

"I seek not his affection," came the reply.

"Then wherefore dost thou show such interest in my husband?" Ana asked curiously.

"Husband?" He asked.

"Aye—husband," she said firmly. "David is my lawful husband, and I am Mistress Colon." She smiled, but not fully just verifying to him he was hers.

"How may this be?" he cried. "For David is already wed—to my own mother." Nathaniel almost looked upset. His face is becoming a bit red.

Henry and Ana just look at him with a combination of confusion and anger. Then they looked at each other.

Chapter IV

How rumors roam the land

Ana and Henry took a walk with Nathaniel and he gave the story of his life with David and his mom. Ana felt hurt and angry that she had fallen for such a man.

Back at the present time

Ana finally made it to her home, feet throbbing and exhausted as well as dehydrated. When she got to the door, no one was there to greet her. She just walked in and walked her way to the bedroom. As she entered her room, she noticed her room door was slightly open, which she has not had it open in a long time since the last issue with David.

She entered the room, walked to her bed, and sat down, slipping her shoes from her feet. A dull throb pulsed through her toes and the soles of her feet. She nudged the shoes beneath the side of the bed, then turned her attention to preparing for a wash. Reaching behind her with her right hand, she found the zipper at the back of her gown and slowly drew it down.

She slipped out of the dress and sank back onto the bed for a moment, only to freeze. Something was on the sheets that hadn't been there before—a dead rooster. Confusion and unease twisted inside her as she reached to move it, and then she saw it: a string tied tightly around its neck. Her stomach sank. It wasn't a random prank. Someone was sending her a warning—a threat of death—as she pressed on with the court case.

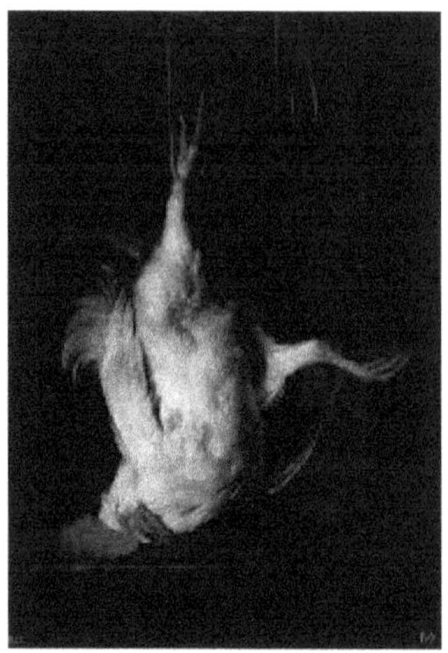

She was angry at first. She threw the rooster against the window and watched it hit the ground.

She then began to pull the sheets off her bed watching blood pour down onto the floor from the rooster.

She then ran into the wash room knowing she was so tired, her feet were throbbing and now she had to deal with this.

She thought about everything she's been through to the lies the things men said to her,now this. She then turned and looked in the mirror above her wash bowl just feeling so overwhelmed . And just sat on her wash room floor and just cried.

She cried for a long time questioning herself should she just let the other stuff go? It was before her, maybe he has changed. Then she asked herself what if he just leaves me as he did the first?

What if he grew weary and abandoned her, leaving her alone with the house and his young children?

She had not seen them since he took the children to another home and instructed the head couple there—Mr. and Mrs. Lucas—that their own household was already burdened by this matter, and that they should not be made to witness whatever consequences this case might bring.

She knew it was meant as yet another reminder of all that could be taken from her, and how even the land itself stood on his side. After a moment of quiet collapse, she wiped away her tears, rose to her feet, and set about cleaning the room. She gathered the blankets and folded them into a corner. When she was finished, she returned to the washroom and washed herself, steadying her breath and her resolve.

She was not going to let anyone stop her from doing what's right. That night she barely ate and fell asleep fast.

The next day

She got ready to face the case and the men who wouldn't care less about what she was being put through.

As she was almost at the courtroom she noticed many people walking towards her. There were about seven women and she noticed two or three of them from the unholy areas.

One woman came straight in front of her. She was light skinned just as pale as milk and hair dark black as charcoal with it looks like a comb and has not been combed in it in a long time.
She had a white dress that was not clean enough to even call white nor off white.

"There be other paths by which one may walk. Perchance I ought to turn again toward my home." She had an attitude and her face showed no shame in facing Ana at this moment.

"Why should I do so? Nay—I shall not return thither." Anna responded as she was not afraid of such a woman.

The women behind the pale one started to move forward to let Ana know they were ready for anything.

"Wherefore trouble thyself with the courts at all? None will lend ear to such base scum.

Thou art branded a hater of men, and thou shalt not prevail." One of the bigger women beside her said out loud. She wore red and black.

She was laced into a corset that accentuated her breasts even more than it compressed her belly. Well over 200 pounds, she wore it confidently, clearly unbothered by any judgment about her body.

"Ladies, I mean thee no offense whatsoever. I must now take my leave and go upon my way." She attempted to go around them as she went to her right another woman went in front of her. She just stared Ana down without saying a word. Ana Just stared back she knew if she didn't show her fears she will have a better chance.

A few seconds later they hear the pale woman say from the side of the group this time.

"Let her pass," said the other.

"By the course this case doth take, she shall soon be numbered among us, if she would but survive." She laughed out loud and the other woman followed her.

The woman stepped aside, allowing her to pass. Ana reached the courtroom just in time, despite the unnecessary encounter with the women of ill repute along the way. The people were filing in, and the judge was moments from taking his seat.

Ana moved to the front of the court, where her table stood beside her lawyer. He leaned toward her and whispered in her ear. As he did, David and his counsel glanced in their direction. Ana felt their eyes upon her, heavy and unyielding.
She turned their way and saw David smiling at her as though he knew something she did not. He then looked back behind him. Ana felt the

need to see what he was looking at and decided to look behind as well.

She then noticed the women she had bumped into earlier that morning. They looked toward him, smiling and waving, while he returned only a faint smile and did not wave back.

The women leaned toward one another,

whispering, before two of them locked eyes on Ana with sharp, accusing glares.

She met their stare, understanding immediately why they were confronting her.

Her husband was relentless, willing to stoop to any measure to make his point. She should have expected him to manipulate the unholy.

Whether he had bribed them or slept with one of them, it didn't unsettle her in the slightest.

The judge finally took his seat and began outlining the case.

"This morn we will proceed in the hearing of the case concerning whether Mistress Ana Colon shall be granted a divorce," He paused for a second and continued. "A matter most rare, for separation betwixt man and wife is scarcely known in law.
Our judgment shall rest upon the charge that Denis Clarke did forsake his lawful wife to consort with another woman, which act standeth contrary to the law, unless sufficient and lawful cause for such betrayal be plainly

shown." He then looks at his team as they nod with agreement.

As they agree David Colon says something out loud.

"Should not my first wife be present to contest this matter? She is not here; therefore, this case ought to be brought to an end forthwith." He bangs his right hand against the table. Making the Judge angry once again.

"Master Colon! Must I put thee in mind of the consequence of thine insolence?" The judge would not tolerate anyone undermining his authority in his courtroom.

This matter is meaningless. Women ought not be given voice, and yet thou persistent in giving ear to these females over a man of good standing, such as Mr. Colon." Jacob Lagoon

stands and yells to the courts for everyone to hear.

The court starts to get rowdy, and we begin to hear people shouting.

"Man-hater! A hater of men!"

"Suffer her not to come near thy men! She shall bring them dishonor and show them no respect!" The unholy woman is ranting to all the other women behind the table. Women start to get us and walk away from fear of what this will bring to them.

The judge starts to realize the courtroom is becoming hysterical. He starts to bang his gavel against his desk. He cannot get ahold of people's attention.

"You must calm down!" He yells. The yelling made it nearly impossible to hear the judge. Frustrated, he signaled the guards to start removing people from the courtroom. As they dragged them out, the judge's voice boomed over the chaos, trying to regain control.

"This case is over for now and will continue early Monday morning, without such people!" He then bangs his gavel again and then walks away from his table and his court clerks escape from the room without being noticed.

Eric, one of the clerks on the courts team, was going into the chamber after the judge and something told him to look back, and he saw Mrs. Colon standing there in distress.

He decided to walk to her to make sure she was okay.

He walks over and her face is so pale and so stressed. Eric feels bad for her thinking if this was his wife how would she be treated.

Could it be this bad? He loved his wife, and it was awful that David would let his wife be treated this way. Even if she wanted out. He must have loved her at some point. So why let it get this far?

"Mrs. Colon, are you well?" He saw a cup of water on the table, picked it up and handed it to her. You can tell she was stressed, her hands were shaking, and she was a bit out of it.

"It is more than I can well endure. I know not what course I ought to take.

Must matters ever remain thus?" She sat down just overwhelmed with what just happened.

"I know the weight presseth sorely upon thee at present, yet thou must go on, for else what profit is there? Madam, thy hand worketh change. Have patience until Monday, and it shall be improved." He said even if he wasn't sure it would be better at all.

"I think it is not so, yet I thank you." She wiped tears that were poured down from her eyes.

Eric gave her a cloth that was in his pocket to wipe her face dry.

"Keep it for thyself. I shall meet with thee on Monday." He touched her shoulder and began walking away into the back room.
As he walked past the exit, a gentleman lingered by the door—it was one of David's friends from the bar.

Ana waited until most of the crowd had left the courthouse before heading home. She'd had enough excitement for one day, and once inside, she crawled into bed and stayed there, motionless, for the rest of the afternoon.

That evening, the courtroom clerk was leaving the saloon, seeking an ale to take the edge off after a long day. With the weekend giving him no early duties, he was in no hurry.

When he climbed into his carriage, he was startled to find a gentleman already seated inside. The shadows made it hard to see him clearly.

"Why are you in my carriage? Do I know you?" Eric asked.

"I think you know my wife quite well." The gentleman moved forward and Eric then realized it was Mr. David Colon from the Courtroom.

"I am not sure what you mean Mr. Colon. May I

ask why would I get such a visit?" The carriage began to go despite his uninvited visitor

.

"Thou knowest full well my meaning. I mark thee, and I hear whisperings that thou art over-near unto her.

The men begin to perceive that if thou standest not with us, then thou standest with them." He then lights up a cigar as he stares at Eric with anger in his eye.

"May I put thee in remembrance that it standeth against the law to beget issues with those of the court?" He knew what

David was doing and found it unnecessary. "As for this talk of them and us, is it helpful at all? I behold naught but a woman who seeketh to be heard, whilst thou and thy band of knaves seem bent, for some cause, on keeping hold of her goods."

He would not let anyone who disrespects his wife faze him in any way.

"Methinks thou dost not rightly apprehend how the order of things doth stand."

"Women are not meant to be heard, and may count themselves fortunate that they are suffering even to be seen." He blew smoke out his mouth from the cigar smoking up the carriage. Eric moves the curtain to open so there is air coming in and the smoke is going out.

"Aye, I recall well hearing such words from Jacob, and I deem him no man thou shouldst be so ready to follow." He then tapped on the side of his carriage letting the one guiding the horse to stop.

"I counsel thee to consider well on which side thou meanest to stand. It shall profit us all if thou dost but fall into order. Thou wouldst do ill to choose amiss, Master Williams." He began exiting the carriage.

Eric was in shock thinking "How came he by my surname? And to whom did he address his words?" He watched Mr. Colon leave and finally felt more at ease but still worried about what's to come.

When he finally made it home his wife was waiting for him at the door with a concerned look.

He thanked the gentlemen for taking him home. "I thank you, sir. May you rest well." The driver nodded and took the horses to the barn. He smiled then walked towards his wife.

After a long day, there was nothing better than returning home to the people he loved.

Eric was deeply in love with his wife.

They had been together for over seven years, and he couldn't imagine being with anyone else. Their happiness had grown even more with the arrival of their new baby boy, Jon.

Eric pressed a gentle kiss to his wife's lips, then to his son, cradled on her hip, feeling that nothing could make him happier.

"A fair sight to ease eyes long wearied." He smiled as they walked into the home.
"Eric, there are whisperings abroad concerning the case before the court. Art thou well?" She was concerned because she heard who was involved in this case and the men that backed him .
"I am well, my love; naught befalls me that I cannot endure. My charge doth require me to contend with such matters."

He smiles trying to hide the fact that he had been threatened in a subtle way.

"Well, I know thou art diligent, yet those men deal in earnest, and thou knowest that that good-for-naught Jacob is concerned. 'Tis no good, Eric." She places the baby in the bassinet. Then goes near her husband to sit by his side.

"Alice, I am well. This matter toucheth not me, but a woman who is sorely wronged and held in contempt. I cannot suffer it to pass, my love. Think, were it thyself."

"I cannot abide the ways of men in this town, nor tolerate that they escape all blame for their misdeeds simply because of their sex," Eric said, shaking his head.

"First and foremost, we shall ne'er find ourselves in such a plight. Thou art bound to me forevermore." She giggled.

"Second, it is for this cause that I love thee: thou hast a heart most gentle, and thou wilt not yield, come what may." She smiled,kissed him and walked to set his dinner.

Chapter V

What should I do?

The next day Eric and his wife went to the market. Their crop was not growing as fast as they would like so they travel to the Market when they need more veggies and herbs to make their meals.

Plus they loved to support other farmers in their land out of respect.

Eric was both a clerk of the office and a Farmer because after his father's past he was left to tend to it but it was not his dream.

He always wanted to make a difference and being in the courtroom even if he was not a judge still meant the world to him.

They walked for about an hour and had a full bag of vegetables and fruits. They were about to head back to the carriage to go home when Jacob showed up in front of them.

"Eric." He said looking at him with an evil smile as the devil himself. Eric knew this was another attempt and he began to get annoyed this time but he knew his wife was by his side so he had to be careful of his moves.

"Jacob." He responded back. Alice began to feel nervous and whispered in his ear.

"We should repair homeward; there is naught more that we need."

"Didst thou not say thou neededst that herb for supper this night?"

"I can do without."She put her head down not to look at Jacob's face as she felt his stare.

"Nay, I pray thee, go fetch thy herb, whilst I speak with thy husband for a moment." Alice looked at her husband on what move to make.

Eric nodded at his wife and she began to walk past them.

"Ay, let the men talk, and see to that which women do best." He said as he laughed.

"Speak not to my wife in such a wise; she is no whore of thine." Eric was so angry at this point he felt himself get closer to Jacob's face to defend his wife if necessary. He felt his hand forming a fist.

Jacob got closer to his face."Boy, thou hadst best know thy place." Two guys came behind Jacob to show his power at the moment.

"I counsel thee to forbear attendance on Monday's labors." He was close in Eric's face; he could smell the Ale just pouring out of his breath.

"And what shall befall me if I do appear?" He knew it wasn't good but he hated the fact that Jacob had the upper hand at the moment.

"Why, we should not wish thy beasts to break loose. I hear gates are often left open. And should some soul take fright and mistake them

for a monster, who can say what might come of it?"

"The poor beasts might lose their lives through such errors, as a fence left unfastened or forgot to be shut." He laughed and the men behind him as well.

Eric was getting more angry and his face was becoming more red. He knew his father would not back down to such a threat but as he was getting ready for the fight of his life he heard a voice.

"Eric, I have fetched my herb; 'tis time we made for home." It was his wife getting his attention to get out of such a mess.

"Ay, Eric, I counsel thee to go home and be the farmer thy father ever meant thee to be." He and his boys go past him and Jacob hits his shoulder which is his own. Knowing at the moment he was not able to defend himself.

Eric stood still, trying to steady himself, when his wife approached and gently took his hand. The softness of Alice's touch grounded him, reminding him of his responsibilities—not just as a man, but as a husband and father.

He looked at her, smiled faintly, and together they began walking home.

Despite not wanting to burden her, he shared what had been happening: the way the woman was treated, the men's behavior, and the threats he had received. He was unsure what to do.

Conflicted, he valued her perspective above all. If she decided he should let the case go, he would—out of respect and trust in her judgment.

They got home and before they left the carriage she looked at him and touched his face with her right palm and said, "My love, I may not bid thee what to do, yet thy heart shall guide thee, and whatever choice thou makest, I shall abide by thy side."

"I shall love thee forevermore, and I shall lead where thou hast need of me." She smiled with so much confidence.

He loved that about her—she never told you what to do, only guided you to the answer you already knew.

They slept through the night until the baby's cries woke Eric. He pressed a gentle kiss to his wife's forehead, then rose from the bed to tend

to their child. Lifting the baby from the bassinet, he stepped quietly from the room.

He had never loved anyone the way he loved his family.

He knew the case would take a heavy toll, and he had to think carefully. Jacob was a powerful man and close to David; when Jacob wanted someone gone, they stayed gone.

Eric held his son a little tighter, determined to protect his family. The day would be spent ensuring their safety, whatever it took.

Back in the colon's home

Ana is fixing herself a basket of food to give herself a picnic of one since it was just such a great day outside.

She was in the kitchen getting bread when one of the maids came to her.

"Ma'am?" One of the maids that used to clean her clothes stood near her.

"Yes, April?" She felt her staring like a child wanting to say something but was too scared to.

"I am right sorry for what Master Colon hath set thee to endure. I do not like it, yet I must see that my family hath food to eat." She put her head down showing sadness with the position she was put in.

April the help, loved Ana after a couple of days of meeting her.

She was outside taking clothes off the line and one flew out of her hands onto the ground. Ana saw this and started walking towards her. April began to be frightened of what could happen to her for dirtying one of the sheets. Instead Ana went up to her and asked her.

"Dost thou need aid…um, what is thy name?" Ana asked.
April was shocked and didn't know what to say other than "I am right sorry, madam; I meant it not." April was nigh to tears. She needed this employment to keep her family from starving.

"Sorry for what? Thou canst no more stay the wind from blowing than keep the sheets from flying where the wind doth carry them."

She smiled and April remembered looking at her and the sun somehow made her glow right behind her.

She grabbed the sheet and took it with her.
"Fear not; I shall carry these myself to be washed." She just walked away as everything was lovely leaving the help in shock.

"Ma'am?" She picked up her basket while looking her way.

"Yes?" She smiled as she looked at her while holding the basket.

"I am known by the name of April." She said knowing Ana was different from others. She didn't treat them like maids but she treated them more like family. Which David did not like at all.

"Tis well, April. I lay no blame upon thee for the harsh judgment that Master Colon hath imposed upon thee." She covered her bread with a cloth, then the maid stocked something else in her basket and smiled.

"A little surprise…hold thy peace and know the younglings speak of you often," She smiled and walked away.   She used to be the lady's maid but now she is Nursery Maid, taking care of the children at night.

Ana grabbed her bag and walked towards the forest area near the river she met her best friend at.

She looked at the river and smiled as memories popped in her head. She grabbed a blanket that was folded in her arm. Ana spread the blanket on the ground and the water.

She grabbed her basket and put it in the corner of the blanket and took her shoes and put it on the other side. She went to sit down when she heard a voice.

"How fair is the water here." It was a woman with dark hair, whose skin tone was fair white. She was a bit over 5 '4 and wearing an olive green dress with white connected to the top.

The dress was very interesting because the green dress sleeves went past her hand almost and were widened at the end. She smiled as the sun shined behind her.

"Ay, indeed. Thou shouldst have seen it in my younger years; it did teeming with algae, so that scarce any might swim therein." She smiled to herself remembering her friend in the water with all that algae on him.

"I would never have thought it." She just stared at the water with amazement.

"I have ne'er seen thee here before. Art thou a visitor from the ships?" She was curious to see such a woman on her land. She would have definitely gotten attention with her beauty.

"I am not of this place; thou art right. Thou mayst not know me, yet I feel as though I know thee passing well, Ana."She looked at Ana but her face was no longer smiling as before.

"I crave thy pardon; I feel somewhat unsettled. How is it that I should know thee?" Ana began to feel like this was another threat that was sent from her husband.

"My name is Charlotte. Thy friend Mark said that here I should find thee this day." She began to take off her shoes and asked.

"May I take a seat?" Ana moved a bit aside to give space to Charlotte to sit by her.

She was curious as to why she was sent to her. If her best friend was sending her it had to be important.

"Well now, thou hast stirred my curiosity. My friend hath ne'er sent any to me but himself. So I must ask, what bringeth thee to this side of the lake?" Ana started taking the food items out of her basket offering some bread to Charlotte.

"Well, thou and I have one person in common, and I think this the only chance we have to speak of what the true matter is." She was

ready to tell Ana what was on her mind and Ana was ready to listen.

"When I first met him, he was but a loving soul. We did take to one another swiftly, and he had the tongue to charm any woman's heart. Ne'er did I see any of what followed coming."

After I was brought to bed of my first child, all these matters came to pass; for David was changed in an instant, as though a light were swiftly quenched or lit." She and Ana talked for what they felt was hours on how they met and how abusive he became to her.

Charlotte discussed how she didn't want him to leave despite his behavior. She begged him to stay; she had a baby and couldn't survive without him.

Ana was shocked hearing these stories about the man she married.

He seemed like a dream come true but she realized she had seen how evil he could become and he was more than just a pretty face with great words.

She felt for this woman and what she had gone through. She could never have let it get that far but every woman is differ from others.

Charlotte stated that David one night let one of his mates take her in her bed against her will.

He demanded she not fight him or there will be consequences. She was raped over and over David even called his son of age seven to show him what a woman is good for. Her son cried and refused to watch.

David yelled and pushed him to the floor and told him he will never be a man if he can't handle such views.

He ran out the room crying, not being able to help himself or his mother.

Ana began to be so angry her face became red as tomatoes. Charlotte just was there with hands on her face and tears running down her cheeks. She felt so useless.

"I am right sorry that thou didst endure such an experience, and had I known, I would not so much as have cast mine eyes upon him. Knowest thou that all believe thee to be dead?" Ana felt the need to tell her because she had a right to know.

"Ay, I know. 'Twas my intent to make the people think thus, for I knew they would ne'er suffer me to depart my land were they aware of the truth."

"David hath a sway o'er folk that thou wouldst scarce believe." She noticed a piece of a pasty in the basket.

Ana took it out of the basket and broke it in half for her and Charlotte."Trust me, I see full well how he hath many here wound about his finger, and how things were shaped to his will ere ever he arrived."

"Thou shouldst bring this matter before the court and tell him plainly what he hath done unto thee." Ana was thinking she can use any help she can get and what better help than the other woman.

"Much as I would wish it so, I must needs remain as one dead.

They would come after me, and I cannot again bring such peril upon myself and my son."

"I came to thee to tell my tale, and he that fighteth for himself is brave indeed; I do envy thee."

"Thy striving doth help me heal, despite what thou mayst think." Charlotte put her plate down with unfinished cake and rose from the blanket placed on the ground.

"Art thou departing?" Ana finally was talking to someone who felt her pain,maybe more.She didn't want her to leave so soon.

"My apologies, I must take my leave before I am noticed. I wish thee all the fortune I can bestow. My son speaks highly of thee, and now I see why—thou art both wise and fair. Pray, enjoy the remainder of thy solitude."

With that, she walked away, and Ana gave a small wave in return.

Ana glanced back at the lake, then heard something and turned toward where Charlotte had been walking—but she was gone, as if she had never been there at all.

Alone, Ana took time to reflect on everything she was enduring and what Charlotte had suffered.

She couldn't fathom that David could be such a man—she had been fooled into loving an evil soul, when usually she could see through people like him.

That evening, she returned home with a resolve: she would fight—not just for herself, but for anyone who had fallen victim to David's deceit.

The next morning, Monday, court would resume. Eric dressed in silence, staring at his reflection as he reconsidered his next move. His wife stepped behind him, straightening the crooked tie at his collar.
The worry etched across his face weighed on her, and she felt a pang seeing him so uneasy.

"My love, thou shalt be well. Since first I met thee, thou hast ever made the right choice, and today thou shalt do no less."

She turned him gently and pressed her lips to his, and he smiled in response. Her words—and her presence—always had a way of soothing him, like the steady rhythm of waves along a quiet beach.

"Love, I know what I must do, yet I must keep my family safe." He sat on bed frustrated.

"How sayest thou, my love, that we and our fair babe should journey today to see my sister for a few days? We shall be safe there." Alice picked up the phone before she dialed and she said one more thing.

"Now do that which thou must; that woman standeth in need of our support." She smiled at him and he smiled back.

He knew what he had to do and knowing his wife would be safe made the decision much easier for him.

Back at the courthouse

Everyone was entering the courthouse getting ready for what they feel is gonna be the entertainment of the day. Mr David felt confident that today would be his day.
He had everyone in his pocket and he knew that he had a better chance then of course Ana did.

He knew that men would not pay attention to her story and he was smiling as he sat at his table waiting for the case to start.

Ana walked in with her lawyer.

He was whispering in her ear as they were walking. He was telling her the things that will occur and what to expect during today's case.

As she was almost at the table she felt eyes looking at her.

It was David smiling towards her way. He smiled and waved and Ana began to get annoyed. She sat and everyone was in the courtroom.

The judge emerged from the back room, followed by his court clerks. One by one, people filed in and took their seats.

David Colon grinned, confident that he had sent his people to influence others to do his bidding. He glanced at Jacob, who winked and gave him a thumbs-up, signaling that the task had been carried out.

When David looked back, Eric was entering last, coming in behind the clerks.

A flush of anger crept across David's face. He shot another glance at Jacob—this time without a smile, only fury.

Before taking his seat, the judge addressed the courtroom with a few opening words.

"This day we shall not suffer this court to be made a mockery. If matters come to such a pass, I shall do one of two things: either have thee put forth from this court, or commit thee to custody for thy disturbance."
Today we will be hearing from the defendant's witness and I expect you to be respectful and listen to his side of the story.

He sat down and grabbed Gavel and tapped the table with it and said "Let's begin."

Chapter VI

His witness

The day was a bit hot and the clerks were beginning to sweat more than just the heat. They all got a visit from Jacob and knew if they took anyone's side but David's that they would be tortured in one way or another.

The judge said to the defendant's lawyer "Let your witness be brought forth at this time." The lawyer nodded to him and said. "I thank you, my Lord."

The lawyer glanced back and nodded toward Jacob Lagoon, signaling him to approach the witness area. Jacob returned the nod with a confident smile and rose to make his way to the front of the court.

He walked with a pride few men of his stature could claim, yet he carried it naturally—proud of who he was and what he had done for his men.

Circling around Ana's table, he reached the witness stand and turned to her with a small, knowing smile before taking the chair he had been instructed to occupy. Another clerk stepped forward with a Bible and asked loudly, "Are you prepared to speak the whole truth, and nothing but the truth, so help you God?"

Jacob looked at the clerk with a laugh and said; "Why, these are the words that pass my lips. Doth such a thing truly exist, or is his name spoken only in the moan of a woman?" He laughed because he didn't believe in God or respected anyone.

"Lagoon, this court hath no patience for thy sport. Take this business in earnest, or quit the chamber at once."The judge said.

"I crave your pardon, Your Honour; I intended no offence." He raised his right hand and placed his left hand on the bible. The clerk knew he would know better than to say a word.

"I have bound myself to utter the whole truth, without guile or concealment, so help me Almighty God." He grinned as he said that.

The clerk then went back to his charity to let the court continue.

The lawyer stood up, looked back at the crowd then looked at Jacob and began to talk.

"Thank you for your presence here today, Master Lagoon."He smiled at Jacob and he responded to it.

"You are heartily welcome." His smile made Ana feel so annoyed but she knew she had to stay calm.

"I have been informed that you have lived upon this land for many years. Is this so, Master Lagoon?" The Defendant's lawyer was getting to court to see how much someone of his stature would need some back story to make him look credible.

"That is so. I have dwelt here since my father brought me unto this land when I was six years of age." He leaned back in his chair, smiling, until his stomach pressed outward against the seat.

"Then, having dwelt here so many years, you are well acquainted with what occurs both within this land and beyond it. Is this so?" The Defendant's Lawyer asked.

"Indeed, thou art correct. Naught escapes my knowledge. I know all who enter and depart, and many things that are done behind closed doors." Ana just looked at him annoyed.

Ana then whispered into her lawyer's ear. He then got up and said to the court.

"I do not understand how this pertaineth to the matter at hand. Is it truly necessary, Judge?" He looked to judge for an answer.

The judge looked at him then looked at the lawyer.

"The defenders;' lawyer answered for him.'Tis needful to declare that if any man knoweth the truth, it is Master Lagoon. I am here to show how much he truly knoweth." The plaintiff's lawyer sat down knowing that trying to fight this war will be harder if he makes a mockery.

"I beseech thee, continue unto Mr. Lagoon." The judge said to him.

"Pray, call me Jacob, Your Honour."

"I would willingly refrain." The judge said firmly.

"Proceed, Master Lagoon. Thou hast so long abided here and art well acquainted with all that transpires upon this land. Pray, how long hast thou known the plaintiff?" The lawyer asked Jacob.

"I have been acquainted with her from the time her father walked this land. He held, or rather did hold, a farm here in Boston." Ana fixed him with a glare, her anger simmering just beneath the surface. He was the same man who had spent so much effort ensuring her father returned home barely able to walk, his words slurred and unsteady.

And now, he was doing the same to her husband, weaving his schemes once more. Around them, everyone seemed to fall into his snare—like flies caught helplessly in a spider's web, struggling with no hope of escape.

"Then, wouldst thou claim to have been acquainted with her for the most part of her days?" The lawyer asked.

"Aye, I think she was as a daughter unto me."

She laughed aloud, earning a stern glance from the judge. She immediately stilled, reminded that he had never considered her as family. In his own deliberate manner, he had always made clear that she was no kin to him.

"Did she ever show defiance whilst growing, or, to put it otherwise, during all the time thou hast been acquainted with her?" He sought to portray her as a defiant wife, suggesting that she was fortunate to have a husband such as Mr. Colon, who would remain with her despite her conduct..

"I think all would agree that she is ever defiant. She ought to follow the rules established upon this land—seen but not heard—yet she is ever one to make herself heard." He gave her a look that he gives his unholy women when they try to talk back to him in any way other than what we expect.

Normally it would end with a slap, but he was the witness in the courtroom. He knew he couldn't risk spending the night in a cell—his woman needed him, and they shouldn't be left alone.

"Pray, canst thou provide an instance of her defiance, particularly against Master David Colon?"

"Verily, I could name many, yet if one must be singled out, it is the occasion when her father was minded to sell me one of his horses—which he had indeed consented to sell me, mind you."

"How is this matter fit for discourse, Mr. Lagoon?"

"Well, I saw her speak to her father as though he were a mere child, which did greatly astonish me, for this gentleman hath cared for her since her mother was no longer among the living." He answered in return.

"And where, Master Lagoon, doth Master Colon have part in this matter?"

"Upon hearing the matter declared, David came forth to witness, whilst I stood observing this refractory woman go back and forth with her father."
He tried to talk to his wife Ana but she refused to hear him or her father and walked away stating out loud. "Should he come by this horse, I will reclaim it, be it by one means or another!" And she just huffed and puffed with anger." As a daughter and a wife no woman should be in such a way."

"Why wilt thou not make known unto them what business thou hadst with the horses?" Ana screamed out loud. "He employed the horses to carry certain physics of his own, goods that are forbidden here."

She was so angry she could not hear any more of his stories and stayed shut.

"Those horses served only to aid the needy, and the physicians can bear witness thereto."

"Thou hast the physicians in thy pocket, Jacob, and thou knowest it well!" Ana screamed and the lawyer tried to keep her calm.

"See that thy client remain calm, lest she sleep this night behind bars." The judge was not going to have the people mess with the rules he had given in the beginning of the day.

"Indeed, Your Honour, I crave forgiveness, for she is greatly stirred in spirit. I shall bring her to order." The lawyer whispered in her ear and she then sat down.

"Behold, Your Honour, she regardeth no man, neither doth she give him due respect." Jacob sought to portray her as a woman who disrespected men, aiming to tarnish her reputation in the eyes of others.

"With the display that Mrs. Colon has shown. What was the outcome for you and receiving the horse?" The lawyer returned to his questions, as if nothing had disturbed him at all..

"I never received him. Somehow she had a hold upon them, and they would rather keep the horse than hearken to her continual nagging." He nodded his head and Mr. Colon was there nodding towards his remark as well.

"Pray, inform the court why her father did at that time seek to sell one of his finest horses." The lawyer possessed knowledge of which she was unaware and was prepared to present this evidence at that very moment.

"Well, he was beset with troubles in his crops, and the weather aided neither fruit nor vegetable. He owed me money, and this was his manner of repaying the debt." He was confident about his answer.

"Lies! They are all Lies!" Ana screamed once again.

"I bid thee set thy client in good order. Take heed, this is the final warning!" By this point, the judge's patience was wearing thin, and his anger was becoming evident.

"Once more, I beg your forgiveness; she shall rise not again to speak."He looked at Ana with anger at this time.

He understood that she would not be heard if she continued with these outbursts.

Ana struggled to maintain her composure, yet Jacob remained relentless, determined to spread falsehoods. She knew, however, that her father was an honest man who would never stoop to such deceit.

"Thou shalt have thy turn to speak, Mistress Colon. Such outbursts prolong this case, and I have many other matters to attend unto." The judge added.

"Will hold my peace, Your Honour." She put her head down.

Then Jacobs responds. "That would be a rare wonder." He laughs when the Judge looks at him and says.

"Mr. Lagoon, continue in such sly comments, and thou shalt be dismissed from the witness stand."

"I am sorry, Your Honour. At times my tongue speaketh ere my mind doth consider."

"See that thy tongue reckon with the consequence of its speech."

"Yes sir!." Jacobs responds.

"Nay, I speak of Your Honour." The judge began to be annoyed with him as Ana was.

"Yea, I crave thy pardon, Your Honour." He said with extra wording.

"Master Lagoon, pray, let us go forward with the matter at hand."

"Yes, let's." He sat up this time.

"If I understand rightly, her refractory manners do cause strife and loss upon this land. Wilt thou concur?" The lawyer said to Mr. Lagoon.

"Yes, that is exactly what I'm saying and we need all the funds we can get trying to keep this land whole." Jacob grabbed his ruffled collar.

"My thanks to thee, Master Lagoon. There is naught further." The lawyer smiled as he sat back at his table.

"We proceed to the questioning of the next witness." The judge says.

"Thank thee, Your Honour." The plaintiff's lawyer got up and approached the Defendant's witness.

"As is known, thou art well regarded for thy labours, but canst thou declare what those labours consist of, Master Lagoon?" The lawyer went straight to the question that will take the witness reputation out in the open.

"Of a truth, I can. Where shall I begin? Hm. I sell goods and render services for the land, and receive funds to maintain it, as I did declare aforetime." he just smiled.

You can tell this was not the first time he has been questioned for what kind of work he does.

"Tell the court, who are they that are served, and who attend unto these clients?" The lawyer needed Jacob to confess on the work he makes the woman do for him.

"I do minister unto the men, but I shall not name them, for they are my clients and are entitled to their privacy."

"Pray, Mr Lagoon, what manner of services dost thou render?"

"I minister to bring comfort unto my clients and to awaken their desires." He grinned widely and the men in the courts laughed a bit. They knew exactly what he meant when he started that because he serviced quite a few of them from time to time.

'Meanest thou not to say that thou dost provide them with women of the night?' The lawyer looked him straight in the eye to see if he would confess.

"They prefer to be known as Masters of Delight in the night hours." He laughed a bit as other men smirched.

"Master Lagoon, take heed; this is the final admonition." The judge said he was smiling because he found it a bit funny but had to maintain order.

"Pray, Master Lagoon, dost that signify a yea?" Lawyer asked.

"What was the question again?"

"Art thy servants indeed courtesans or women of that sort?" He said sternly to let him know he meant business.

"In words, yea; yet their affronts extend far beyond mere speech."

"And the clients, thou dost also provide them with physic from thy workers, dost thou not?" The lawyer wanted him to say it but knew Mr. Lagoon would not make it for them or the court.

"Maybe." Jacob was starting to shut down saying less because he knew he would know the more he gave the more in trouble he would be.

"Only a yea or nay, Master Lagoon."

"Yes."

"Dost thou reckon that many upon this land do fear thee in some manner?"

"I wouldn't call it fear." he smiled once again.

"And what, then, wouldst thou call it?"

"I would say we all hold understanding, and they do take my rules into consideration."

"And what befalleth those who take not thy rules seriously, Master Lagoon?"

Jacob was starting to get more annoyed by these questions and he felt as though he was on trail.

"I stand not upon trial. David, pray, why am I so vexed?"

"In what manner art thou harassed, Master Lagoon? We ask naught but in our office as counsel, for it behoveth us to discern if thy words are trustworthy."

"No one shall question me. Your Honour, I beseech thee, suffer me to withdraw." Jacob says everyone starts to become annoyed and starts talking and complaining out loud.

"May he do such a thing, Your Honour?" David stood up to try to get his only witness to stay and defend him.

"He may, yet he must know that all which he hath spoken shall be stricken from the record. Unless thou hast another witness, thou shalt have none to defend thee but thy counsel. Is this thy true desire, Master Jacob Lagoon?"

They stared at him and he stood back thinking what was worth this trial.

Was it worth David's partnership he promised him or was it something that will give too much light to this in the dark business.

Chapter VII

Her witness

It became very quiet waiting for his response. The judge asked again.

"Dost thou wish to withdraw from the witness seat, Master Lagoon?"

Jacob glanced toward the judge, then shifted his gaze to David, whose anger seemed on the verge of bursting from him. If looks could speak, this would have been a warning to stay in line and fulfill his duties. He drew a deep breath and finally spoke: "I withdraw, Your Honour.." He looks so beat and says to David.

"I dare not put my good name at risk to save thine."

He gets up and walks off the witness stand.

He passes the both sides and he doesn't look either side raises his head and just begins to walk out the court as 3 woman, two men join him as he exits. Those who follow him are his workers.
"How now, darest thou so? This matter shall not rest!." David yelled to him as the lawyer was trying to calm him down.

The judge realized that he needed a drink and to take a breath. "Let us take a short while to set ourselves in order that we may proceed. We shall resume again in twenty minutes." Everyone starts to walk out the courtroom.

This time Ana was out before David since he needed to be talked to about his outburst.

It took everyone an hour to get back to the court calm and ready for the next witness. Everyone remained quiet and just waited for the judge to say it was time to continue.

"I am not ignorant that passions run high at this time; yet we must call to mind that such outbursts do but lengthen the case, which, methinks, hath already endured long enough. Are you not of the same mind?" Judge Matthew said.

Everyone nodded or said yes quietly.

"So be it; let us proceed forthwith and resume these proceedings." He then hits his Gavel against the table and everyone gets ready for the next witness.

"Your Honour, I stand ready to call forth my witness." The plaintiff's lawyer said to the judge.The judge nods.

Moments later, a witness appeared from behind them. Nathaniel Colon stepped forward to the witness stand. He was the son of David Colon—a man who had known him only as a baby and had never truly seen what he looked like until now. David was taken aback, struck by how strongly Nathaniel resembled his mother.

Nathaniel then took his seat, facing his father's new wife and the gathered courtroom. Some attendees wore expressions of confusion, unsure of his identity, while others bore looks of anger. The only person smiling was Ana, for she knew Nathaniel would speak the truth.

He carried himself with the courtesy of a gentleman toward Ana and held no ill will toward her.

"We give thee our thanks, Nathaniel, for thy attendance this day." The lawyer started politely.

"You are most welcome." Nathaniel smiled as he was ready for anything. He knew being his son they would not go easy on him.

"Pray, explain unto the court how thou art connected to Master David Colon."

"Yea, indeed. He is my father." Many shocked faces and whispers made their way around the courtroom.
"Is thy mother called Ana Colon?" the lawyer asked to make sure they knew Ana was not related to Nathaniel at all.

"Nay, sir. I possess my own mother. No disrespect be meant to the gracious Ana."

"Tell the court, what is the name of thy mother?" The lawyer had to go through the steps to make sure he did everything correctly. He had no wiggle room for mistakes.

"The name of my mother is.." He paused for a second while we looked at Davids Colon to make sure he heard her name and remembered it. "My mother is called Charlotte Colon." He sat up more directly to show he will not bow down to David and he will tell the truth.

"By thy words, Charlotte Colon, dost thou imply that she hath kinship with Master David Colon?" This is where the lawyer will make sure the truth would be heard.

"Charlotte,my mother, is likewise his wife." Whispers began around the room once again.

"Tell the court, how long were thy mother and he together before he forsook his family and traveled to this land?"

The began pushing in the knife of information a bit more so he could feel what was about to happen.

"By my mother's account, he departed from us whilst I was four years of age. So long hath it been that my remembrance is scarce, and only small bits of him linger in my mind."

"Why did thy father resolve to depart? Or did thy mother not discourse of this with thee?"

"As I was told, he did but decided one day to leave, and returned no more."

"So, is that all thy mother hath told thee concerning thy father?"

"Nay, she told me he was not a good man, and did not know how to treat a woman rightly." Nathaniel looked at his father with a bit of resentment.

He had heard many stories but chose not to discuss them, knowing it would only fuel anger and that he was not yet ready to reveal to his father the power his words could have over him.

"I object!" David shouted, his voice cutting through the courtroom. All eyes turned toward him, including the judge's, filled with confusion. He was no lawyer—he had no right to interject.

"Thou art not permitted to raise objection, Master Colon. That right belongeth solely to thy lawyer.." He smiled politely.

David leaned over to his lawyer and whispered in his ear.

"Your Honour, pray, might we withdraw for a short space to speak privately?" The lawyer asked politely.

The judge nodded. Letting both lawyers come forward. They were whispering so the rest of the court could not hear.

"May it please Your Honour, is this person to be deemed a credible witness, or merely a spiteful child abandoned of old?" The defendant's lawyer asked.

"He is no way scornful; he merely propounds the questions I would pose, and that is all." The Plaintiff's lawyer answered back.

"What purpose serveth these questions? They pertain not at all unto the plaintiff."

"It behoveth us to know wherefore he left and did take another wife, in all matters concerning which Ms. Colon is involved."

"It is understood, Counsel. Save thou hast other objections concerning this witness, we shall continue.." The judge fixed his gaze on the defendant. He returned a look to his client, then back to his lawyer, seeming at a loss for words.

"No, your honor."

"Very well, we will continue forthwith.." Both lawyers looked at each other then looked at the judge nodded and headed back to where they were before.

"As I spoke before, Master Colon, thy mother did say he was not a man of virtue. Is this so?"

"Yes,that is correct."

"I do protest, Your Honour. This conversation lacketh proof and is mere hearsay."

The judge cast his gaze toward him, seemingly ready to side with the defense lawyer, when the sound of the courtroom door opening drew everyone's attention. A middle-aged woman entered. All eyes turned toward her, uncertain of her identity—except David. When he saw her, his face went pale.

"This is not hearsay, Your Honour. He speaketh the truth!" A woman speaks up, in a teal and white formal dress consisting of the stiff-bodiced mantua.

She came down the aisle ready to speak to the court and nothing could stop her.

"Ma'am, and who art thou, coming into my courtroom thus to be disruptive?" The judge questioned the woman, his tone sharp, as if his authority in the courtroom were being challenged in front of the clerks and all present.

Progress had finally been made in the case, and now this disruption seemed to test the judge's patience to its limits. How much could one man endure?

"Forgive me, Your Honour, yet I may not allow my son to speak on my behalf." Everyone whispered and all you heard was shocked sounds from the whole courtroom.

"Do you say that you are his mother? I was given to understand that you were no longer in this world." The judge began to question the whole case at this point.

"These alliterations are false." The defender's lawyer spoke out.

"These allegations are not false. I spoke with her, and know assuredly that she is Nathaniel's mother." Ana spoke up.Despite her inner turmoil and the risk of facing further scrutiny, she carried herself with quiet pride as she entered the courtroom—determined to stand in support of her son and defend his honor and integrity.

"He is my son, and David my husband. I am come to lay forth the whole of this matter ere thou dost pass judgment upon the life of this most respectable woman."

"Your Honour, may the witnesses now be called forth and exchanged?" The plaintiff's lawyer asked.

"Well, if she doth indeed know the whole of the tale, the least we may do is grant her a hearing." The Judge said as there were confused faces and whispers all around.

This was never heard of before and no one in that courtroom had any idea to expect.

The judge leaned toward the court clerk at his side and spoke in hushed tones, seeking counsel on how best to proceed. Their quiet exchange lasted no more than three minutes, though to those waiting, it felt far longer. The courtroom remained still, anticipation thick in the air as all awaited his decision.

At last, the clerk resumed his seat, and the judge straightened, preparing to address the court.

"Being the lawful wife, she shall be permitted to stand forth as the witness in place of another." There were upsetting noises and angry faces on the defendant's side.

David knew that if she was to speak his reputation would be tarnished for sure.

He thought maybe if he made a distraction he could get the judge to postpone the case one more day and then he could make she his wife stay dead.

He looked back at one of his men that worked (Also known as a hitman) for him and nodded. The man he was nodding to was one of his Regicide. He met him through Jacob and has been working for him ever since.

The hit man then took one of the men in front of him and grabbed him by the neck. The woman near him screamed for help.

"Help him! Give succour! They choke my husband!" All of the courtroom turned around and looked at what was happening in the back. In shock.

The courtroom deputy rushed forward, moving swiftly toward the man who was choking the gentleman. He seized him firmly and dragged him out of the courtroom, restoring order as the victim and his wife followed to ensure he was unharmed.

The judge surveyed the room, noting that the commotion had begun to subside and that calm was slowly returning to the court.

"I know not what hath transpired here, yet we must proceed. I have no further days to devote to this cause." The judge resumed speaking as the deputy reentered the courtroom and offered a subtle nod, signaling that the situation had been handled.

David's frustration grew; his options were dwindling, and the judge showed no sign of yielding. Determined to see the matter through, the judge remained firm in his resolve to proceed with the case.

Order was restored as everyone returned to their seats, and the proceedings began once more.

"Mrs. Colon, can you endure to continue?" the lawyer asked. She nodded and said "Yes. thank you"

Charlotte straightened in her seat, prepared to be questioned and to speak her truth.

"I thank thee. The man who standeth before me is not the man I once believed I knew."

She turned her gaze toward David, and he lowered his head.

"The man I came to know was base and filled with contempt. There was not an innocent bone within him."

David's head lifted in shock at her words, startled that no one rose to silence her.

"I have known David these fifteen years and more. We were raised together, our fathers laboring in company. Both our fathers were the heads of a certain club, a night-house of exclusive men, named the 'Old Colony Club for Men."
"It was on one such occasion, when both our parents entertained at their club and required our aid in bearing things thither, that we first met."

"From that instant, all was changed. We became friends, and as time wore on, something more. Yet as the days passed, I beheld him threaten other lads, though I gave it no heed, thinking ever that boys would be boys." The lawyer interrupted.

"In what manner did he threaten these boys?"

"I object." David's lawyer shouted out before Charlotte could answer.

"Wherefore do you object? 'Tis a question of simplicity. We aim to gather knowledge to prove that he was a bully from his earliest years."

"This question is but hearsay; she was not party to that affair and cannot truly know the course of it." The defendant's lawyer was not trying to put more stories to let his client look worse than he already does.

"This is no hearsay; he himself did tell me in person wherefore he had so bullied that child." Charlotte spoke up.

She resented the implication that she was being dishonest. She had come to speak the truth, and this was the only opportunity she would be given—whatever the consequences might be.

The plaintiff's Lawyer looked at her and asked "What caused the defendant to pick upon these children, Mrs. Colon?"

"When I asked him what was amiss, he stated his father sent him to attend that boy, for his father owed him money and had not yet paid the same." She said straight out without hesitation.

"Art thou saying that his father was a man given to swindling?" He asked firmly,because if she is to accuse David she must be precise in her wording.

Chapter VIII

The him no one knew

"I say only that his reply did then incline my thoughts, yet I suffered it to pass without further challenge."

"At what time did Master Colon begin to show forth his true nature?"

"I object! This is but conjecture," The David lawyer shouted out.
"Sustained."

"Then suffer me to frame the question anew. Mistress Colon, did David alter his carriage toward thee during the time ye lived together as man and wife?"Ana's lawyer glanced toward opposing counsel, as if anticipating another objection.

Receiving none, he turned his attention back to Charlotte.

"Aye, yet not for the better." Charlotte looked at David then looked at Ana. Ana nodded her head as she knew what was about to come and she wanted to let Charlotte know it's okay to tell the truth.

"What dost thou mean, not for the better?"

"It signifieth that he began to regard me as though he were mine own father, and I a debtor bound unto him."

"I pray thee, make this plainer for the Court. In what manner did his father deal with others?"

"It is thus:in the first days he would cry out against me, and I did persuade myself that his father had shaped him so, and therefore I bore it. Would God I have not suffered it to proceed so far." Her face seemed ashamed.

"He then fell to railing at me for trifles, such as my failing to meet him at the appointed hour. And thereafter, if I did not straightway comply with his demands, he would lay hands upon me and thrust me aside." She looked at David with unrestrained anger, scarcely believing she had ever allowed him to reduce her to a victim.

"How far did this cruelty extend?" He looked around and said for the court to hear "For that which thou describest is known in law as abuse."

"Your Honor." David's lawyer looked at him to make him stop using the word abuse because it will hurt his case.

"Denied, counsellor. Proceed, Mistress Colon" he nodded to Charlotte.

"Thank you. Your Honor." The plaintiff's lawyer responded. David looked at his lawyer very upset and a part of him was wishing he would have represented himself.

"His behavior grew so grievous that he would strike me upon the face, and afterward beg pardon, as though he had but broken a teacup or some such trifle, saying he meant it not, that his anger had mastered him. Such were the excuses he offered each time he laid his hand upon me." All you heard behind the lawyers were gasps from the women and whispering.

"As the Court may plainly discern, this is abuse, and therefore this cause, and the testimony Mistress Charlotte hath given, ought to be received with the utmost gravity." Ana's lawyer looked and addressed the court. Then turned back around to ask another question.

"You may continue." He started to talk to Charlotte.

"I would fain say that it ended as swiftly as it began, yet such was not the case. He suffered his companions to affront me likewise, deeming it sport, and permitted them to utter names no gentlewoman ought to hear."

The lawyer then said, "I wot it is grievous to recount, yet canst thou give us an example, that the court may ken what vile words thou wast fain to endure from these wretched folk?"

Charlotte glanced at Ana once more, seeking reassurance. Though nervous to recount the events, she understood that she must. Having sworn to tell the truth, she held deep respect for the court and its authority.

"They would utter words such as 'harlot' or 'strumpet.'" Tears began to run down her face.
"I am most sorrowful; that must needs have grievously pained thee. To hear such vile speech may mar both a lady's honour and her mind." He grabs the clothes from his pocket and gives it to her.
"I do object. That is no question, but mere assertions void of proof."

The judge paused, weighing whether the objection merited consideration. He glanced toward his court clerks, silently seeking their counsel. One by one, they nodded in agreement.

He then turned forward, composed himself, and spoke.

"Sustained. Proceed, good counsel, and pose thy question." The judge said firmly.

"I crave thy pardon, Your Honour. I shall reframe it into the form of a question."
The Defendant's lawyer then walked back to his desk and looked at his files for a second then walked back to the witness.
"Mrs. Colon."

"Yes." She responded.

"Didst thou feel.." He paused for a second to ask it correctly. "Didst thou feel thyself grievously afflicted by the actions of Mr. Colon toward thee?"

Mr. Colon looked at his lawyer once again. David could not believe what he was allowing at this time.

"Indeed, I do, and verily, I did." she said as she looked towards Mr. Colon's direction. Showing she is not afraid anymore.

"Canst thou recount further the comportment of Mr. Colon, and how he did treat thee in those days?"

"Verily. As time wore on, David grew more cruel, permitting his companions to treat me in like manner; yet it was not alone in words that they did affront me." She was ready to let them all know what he was really like behind closed doors.

"Canst thou be more particular in thy meaning when thou sayest 'not by words alone'? to the court please."

"It began upon a certain night when I was nigh in slumber. I lay in my bed, clad in my nightgown."

"As I lay upon my bed, nigh in slumber, I felt a presence creep unto me.

I deemed it David, for who else would enter a wife's bed but her husband? I kept mine eyes closed, and anon felt a hand tracing upon my legs unto my thighs. I was sore amazed, for my husband had touched me not these many months."

"Sayest thou, then, that he suffered thee not to perform thy wifely duties to content him, whilst he did oppress thee both in body and in mind?" The lawyer asked to verify how hurtful that must have been to her.

"Yea, after he struck me upon divers occasions, I bore bruises upon sundry parts of my body. I can scarce suppose he found me comely with such marks upon me."

"We give thee thanks for imparting so intimate a matter. Pray, continue thy discourse."

A hush fell over the courtroom, thick and expectant, as all eyes turned to Ana, waiting to hear what she would say next about David.

The spectators were already reeling from what had been revealed—what more could she possibly add about a man who had already shown himself capable of both physical cruelty and the quiet, corrosive torment of the mind? Behind closed doors, such things might remain hidden, whispered only in fear and shame. But here, in the open air of the courtroom, before so many witnesses, every word she spoke carried the weight of truth laid bare—a devastating clarity of what had truly been endured.

"After a brief while, I felt his hands upon my bosom, and anon I perceived that it was not my husband's hands that did touch me." She thought about how it may make her feel when that happens. She became saddened.

"Though he be a most grievous man, yet in the beginning he bore himself as a gentleman in our acquaintance, and this did not feel as his hands had felt before. There was another man, and the scent of ale did cling to him and linger upon me." She was grabbing a piece of her dress because her palms became clammy and a bit wet, she needed to dry them.

All you heard was gasp and David trying not to look at his first wife at that time. Feeling foolish and not ashamed but did not want others to know what had been happening.

"That must needs have been most fearful. Who, then, was this man that was not thy husband?" The lawyer asked with a concerned look for her.

"I was uncertain in that moment, and sought only to free myself from beneath him. He seized me, thrust me down, and did say—"

"I have paid the price, and thy husband doth say thou art mine this night." A tear started to run down her face. Too many memories for her to recall.

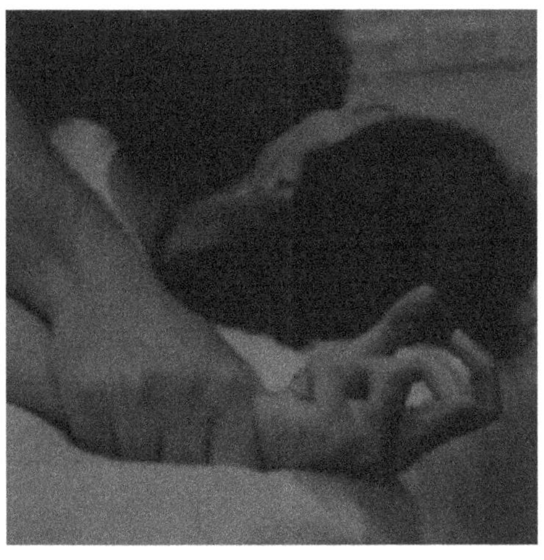

"I am deeply grieved to hear it. Dost thou aver that thy husband, Mr. Colon, was recompensed by that man to deliver thee unto him for carnal favour upon that night?" Whispers were everywhere at this point.

Some men were smiling while others with their wives grabbed their wives or sat closer to their wives by that point.

The men holding their wives were thinking they can never let their wives be touched by anyone other than themselves.

Most of the wives started off as virgins and if they were not they would be not considered to be wife material and be unwedded most of the time.

"Such were the words the man did utter as he lay upon me, treating me as though I were some profane woman of the streets.

He kept me so for much of the night; I recall crying aloud in anguish, and he did cover my mouth, bidding me be silent that he might attend to his own vile intent." Charlotte looked at Ana for comfort but Ana was looking at David with such anger but did not say a word.

"Alas, I am greatly sorrowed that thou wert made to endure such cruelty. What words did thy husband speak when that vile man had finished his deed?"

"After he was done with me, he departed; and my husband entered the chamber as I sat alone, weeping bitterly." She paused for a second still in such shock of these words. And then continues. "Then he said unto me, 'Next time thou hadst best hold thy peace, else I shall sew thy mouth shut."

She then said, "I could scarce believe it, being struck with shock and heavy shame. How could he suffer such a thing to befall me? Wherefore doth this evil come to pass?" Charlotte began to cry and The lawyer brought her another tissue to wipe her tears.

"As you may plainly discern, this poor woman was abused not alone in body and in mind by her husband, but further violated by strangers. My client, Ana, doth only now begin to suffer the lasting effects of this so-called gentleman, so well regarded by many." The lawyer looks around and points straight at David and continues to say.

"We must therefore consider what fate awaits her, should she be bound to remain in marriage with such a vile man." As the lawyer is looking David puts his head down with shame and embarrassment.

"Many thanks to thee, Charlotte, for granting us a glimpse of what it might be to be wed unto Mr. Colon." The lawyer ends his questioning.

"I know full well it could not have been easy to live through it once more." She nodded and she noticed David talking to his lawyer. Before Charlotte could get up the defendant's lawyer shouted out to the judge.

"Your Honour, might I be granted leave to cross-examine the witness? I would put a few questions to Mistress Colon myself." The defense's attorney asked.

"You may." The judge agreed.

"Thank you, your honor." The lawyer wanted to see if he could change the narrative of what Charlotte said by asking specific questions that will make her look bad instead.

Ana's lawyer sank into his seat, allowing David's counsel the floor to pose his questions. He felt a quiet confidence, certain that the defense would falter long before any real challenge could take hold—especially after Charlotte's piercing testimony had already laid bare the extent of David's behavior.

"Good afternoon, Mrs Colon." The lawyer started off nicely to show he has some manners.

"Good afternoon." She knew not to trust him; he was defending the only man in her life that could destroy her life.

"It was reported unto me by many that Mr. Colon's wife was no longer among the living." Charlotte just looked at him then looked at Ana. Ana then whispered to her lawyer and then the lawyer said "Object, he is stating Hearsay."

The judge responded "Sustained, counsellor; I hear no question put."

"I was about to come to that, Your Honour." The judge nodded. "If you lied and claimed yourself dead, what assurance have we that you now speak the truth?"

"I am." She began to get angry. She knew it was the truth she went through and was not an easy thing to even talk about yet she came today and told her story so others could hear the truth.

"And by what means should this court know whether you desired to lie with that man? Perhaps your husband knew nothing of it at all, and perhaps, as with the lies of your past, you now deceive us again."

"Your Honour, he doth interrogate the witness, who is not upon trial before this court. It is David Colon who stands accused." Ana's lawyer shouted out. He knew what David's lawyer was trying to do and he would not stand for it.

"I seek only to know if she may be trusted, Your Honour." David's lawyer responds back to Ana's lawyer.

"Proceed." The judge wanted to see where this would be going after all we only knew of her today.

"Thank you." He looked back at Charlotte and asked another question because he just wanted the court to question her story.
"Mrs Colon. You did state that your husband desired not to lie with you for the sake of your bruises; is this so?"

"Yes, the sight of them displeased him greatly." Her head went down out of embarrassment, it made her feel ugly and it was embarrassing that her own husband would not even look her in the eye.

"I am sorry, Mrs. Colon, yet I find it difficult to credit that a husband should refuse to lie with his wife. Verily, we men are not so choosy, but take what is offered." The lawyer turned around looking at the men of the court to see if any man would deny it.

"Am I right?" A ripple of laughter passed among the men in the courtroom, rough and careless. To them, it seemed no great sin to indulge in desire, so long as a woman showed interest.

Even the judge allowed himself a brief, almost imperceptible chuckle—but the sound faded quickly, and the solemnity of the court returned, settling like a heavy cloak over the assembly. "Counsellor, thou art venturing into deadly waters." The lawyer turned back to Charlotte to continue. "Mrs. Colon, I would ask thee: Is it not your desire to lie with your husband instead?" The lawyer asked.

"Of a truth, it was not my desire. I did strive many times to give him satisfaction, yet he would feign to wish to lie with me; but when I began to unlace my corset, anon his desire would flee." She did not hesitate to tell the truth.

"If the courtesy did keep him content, why remove it? Surely, if thou wouldst be intimate with thy husband, it should help; am I correct?"

"In truth, I would not object, but the corset is not easily endured at such a time with my husband. How should it end well, if I lay like a corpse? To be bound so fast and unable to stir would delight no soul."

"What I hear is this: you refused your husband what he clearly desired. You denied him as a man. And if such accounts be cast aside, I ask anew: how are we to know that all other tales you tell are true?"

Charlotte goes to respond to that and the lawyer interrupts..

"I rest my case, and offer my thanks unto thee,

Mrs. Colon." and the defense lawyer walks away.

There were whispers and the court talking to each other on what to do now.

The judge said for the court to hear. "Let us take a short while to deliberate and rest. These proceedings shall resume in twenty minutes."

Chapter IX

Facing the demon himself

The men of the chamber gathered in small clusters, their voices rising as they debated the next course of action. The discussion grew boisterous, laughter and sharp opinions mingling, and many reached for glasses of whiskey, the amber liquid catching the light as it passed from hand to hand, lending warmth to their heated deliberations.

"Come now, lads, compose yourselves. We must give thought to what course we shall take in this matter. What say you? Where do we stand, and how ought we to proceed henceforth?" The judge says out loud , drawing the room's attention. "Time grows short," he said, his voice firm.

"You must weigh carefully each move you make, for no course is without peril. A single misstep, and all may go awry, regardless of intent."

Clerk one says "We must choose our kind with care, else it shall in the end bring our reputation to ruin."

Clerk two responds "Who is to say it be not already undone, merely by our taking up this case at all?"

Clerk three "I am much in doubt whether we ought to pursue this case any further. Whichever way it fall, it bodes ill, and may touch not only ourselves but the course of the next election. What if our next mayor should be a woman?"

The men laughed among themselves, remarking that there had never been a man in the elections, only the wives standing behind the men they supported. Their voices echoed through the chambers as they debated strategy, unconcerned with the eyes of the court beyond.

Outside, the rest of the court took a moment to breathe, to step away from the tension that had gripped the room. Ana and Charlotte lingered together, speaking in quiet tones, sharing thoughts and seeking comfort in each other's company while the storm of proceedings carried on behind the heavy doors.

"Ana, much as I take pleasure in thy company, notwithstanding the place we find ourselves, thou must pardon me; I have need to retire to the powder room." Ana grabs Charlotte's hands

and starts walking away towards the powderroom.

They were walking towards the end of the hall where David exited the men's room zipping his unzipped pants.

Charlotte quickened her pace, hoping to slip past David unnoticed, but he stepped directly in her path, cutting her off. She froze, heart hammering, as her gaze met his—dark, cold, and unyielding. In that instant, she saw the very demon she had feared, the one she had tried to avoid by staying away altogether. Every instinct told her to flee, yet she was rooted to the spot, forced to confront the threat she had long anticipated.

Charlotte tried to walk a bit faster to get out of David's way but he approached in front of her and blocked her way.

Charlotte froze, she was looking the demon in his eye and this is why she did not want to come in the first place because she knew it was testing what this demon or others would do to her.

"For one said to be dead, thou dost seem most lively indeed." He smiled at her knowing she was scared of him.

He enjoyed the fear he left on her face, as he loved it on anyone else who he can control. His smirk annoyed Charlotte.

"Stand aside, David." Charlotte tried to move around him again.

"Fear not; thou shalt not seem alive again. Of that I shall make certain." Ana noticed what he was doing and made her way over to them.

As Ana got closer she spoke out loud to David. "I pray thou hast not forgotten how to find the gentleman's chamber yonder." He just looked at her with hate.

"Nay, merely offering my greeting unto my wife. Am i not entitled" He looked back at Charlotte, smiled and let her go into the ladies room.

"Which one." Ana said sarcastically.

"Well, most certainly not thee. Thou wouldst not even have me as thy wife, dost thou not recall?" The demon in his eyes wanted to choke her but refrained from doing so because of where he was. He just balled his fist and then let go.

"She desires not to be thy wife likewise. She did feign her death to escape thee.

Perchance thou shouldst take a hint thereof." She rolled her eyes at him. She will not make him feel anything but small because that's what he deserved.

"Count thyself fortunate to stand even in my presence. And think not that I am ignorant of my servants granting thee their regard. Should they be found hanged for having betrayed me at thy bidding, the weight of it shall rest upon thy conscience, not upon mine." He smiled and walked away.

Ana could not stand him and knew he was just talking but glad he walked away. She started to think to herself. He needed them no one else would work for him because of his reputation at the moment. He wouldn't even know how to feed himself without his servants.

Ana then walked into the powder room to check on Charlotte to make sure she is okay after seeing David. Ana knew that it would be a lot on her. As she walked in she noticed that no one was in front of the mirror.

Then she called out quietly thinking she might be using the toilet. "Charlotte?" No answer. "Charlotte?" again No answer, she then looked down under the two doors. Charlotte was nowhere in sight. Ana was thinking to herself.

"Where might she be, and at what moment had she the chance to slip away unseen?" Ana then walked out of the bathroom and looked in the halls for her. No sight whatsoever of her.

Ana decided to start heading to the courtroom because they are running out of time.

Two minutes later she was walking into the courtroom and looked around still no sight of her. She then walked to her friend to ask if he had seen her. He nodded no.

Everyone was sitting back in their seats. Her mind started to worry about Charlotte and wondered if David had to do anything with her being gone.

She went back to her table but she stared towards David's way with anger. Thinking all sought bad things.

The judge and everyone sat it sounded so quiet waiting for what the judge was about to say.

"My councilman and I have conferred, and this cause hath endured far longer than it ought.

Three weeks have passed, and we have suffered foul speech, ill comportment, and quarrels even amongst our own companions."

"Thus shall I suffer the attorneys to deliver their final testimony, setting forth their side of the matter, and thereafter we shall render our judgment." Before he could finish what he was saying the courtroom doors opened and Charlotte strolled in with her head held high.

Ana was relieved she was okay. Charlotte walked and sat behind Ana's table as the judge continued.

"As I spake erewhile, the attorneys shall deliver their final testimony, setting forth their several sides of the matter, and I shall give my judgment thereafter.

Have ye any questions before we proceed?"
No one said a word.

"Let us proceed. Today we shall begin with the Defendant's side; thereafter the Plaintiff may make their closing."

"Thank you, your honor." He whispered something into his client's ears, grabbed his file, took a second to look at it and then stood up to state his testimony.

"Pause awhile, that ye may cast thine eyes upon my client." They all turn and look at David and the lawyer's hand gesture for them to look.

"He is not only a man of comely appearance, but he hath lent a helping hand ever since he set foot upon this land." David nodded for the compliment.

The Lawyer continued. "Yet the Plaintiff doth allege he hath committed grievous deeds, though she hath left certain matters untold."

"How he hath aided her and her father throughout the year, striving to make their farm prosper."

"She likewise spoke not of how kindly he hath been unto his child. All did fix upon the ill and that which he failed to do, yet he received no commendation for his goodness."
"He discharged his duties as a man ought, without murmur or complaint." He then turned back at the judge and the rest of the council.

"I would say, here this cause began, that Mistress Colon was content and living the life which all women might wish to enjoy. He made companions and grew greatly esteemed among those who served him."

"Why would any woman seek to forsake so good a man for a mere rumor, which hath not only sullied his name but cast a shadow upon his reputation for deeds of the past?" He looked around and he saw some faces that seemed to agree with him. He smiled.

"Now I do conclude with these words: Is this cause truly needful, or but a device to gain more notice as a wife?" He then returned to his table and spoke, "I thank you."

Ana felt like he was convincing the whole court that he was a good man and she couldn't understand why they would believe him?

It was the plaintiff's turn for their testimony and they knew they had to do a great job to even top the Defendant's testimony. The lawyer has a good rep and knows how to sway the courtroom easily.

Before the lawyer got up to talk Ana grabbed a pen and a piece of paper and wrote something on it and handed it to her lawyer. He then looked at it and nodded.

The lawyer stood up and walked around his desk to represent the whole court.

"Good afternoon to all present this day, and to the council. I give thanks that ye do take this cause with such earnestness." He heard some Good afternoons back. Then continued.

"Much as I wish we were met here for mere pleasantries, such is not the case.". He repeated,"We are not. We are here, despite what Mr. Colon doth show of his comely appearance and his feigned betrayal of that man whom men do look unto."

"We are met to declare the truth of why we have been thus occupied for these past three weeks. He hath not only deceived his wife, but hath likewise forsaken his former wife. He treated them both unjustly, and oppressed them unto submission."

"Yet my client was beguiled by his wiles; the wall, however, did yet stand, and shall no longer endure such affronts."

"He was so cunning in his deceits that we perceived not the bruises hidden from view. So skilled was he in portraying himself a good man that we marked not how he bade his servants place dead beasts in my client's bath.

So great was his artifice that we overlooked how he compelled the wife he professed to love to walk many miles home these past three weeks, for that she would not yield her right to be the first and only wife. He hath taken from her both her servants and her only son, jesting, as he said, 'it was for her own good.'". Whispers came into the room. The woman began looking at David angrily.

"As all women are taught by their parents that they should seek no more than what their husbands provide, yet what if he doth seek elsewhere?"

"What if the only boon he bestoweth be naught but mental torment and bodily harm? Where are the laws against such? Where is justice for their good name, wrested away for desiring naught but a quiet and happy marriage? Therefore, ere ye judge of tales that may hide the truth, I counsel you to ponder your own lives, and the wives ye hold."

"Consider how ye would treat them, as the wives or mothers of your children, with due respect. All my client doth ask is this: if she hath parted from one who deceived her, abused her, and hath another wife, is it not for something better—a better man, or at least a better life?" He walked back to his table and closed by saying.

"I thank you for your ears and for the time ye have lent."Her lawyer ended arguing his case. He sat down, looked at Ana nodded his head to her and nodded. Ana smiled back at him and looked back at Charlotte and smiled with her as well.

Everyone looked at Ana and Charlotte with kindness. The ladies felt hopeful and are hoping that is enough to convince the rest of the court.

The judge rose from his seat, the gavel still in hand, and spoke with measured authority. "My counsel and I shall take time to deliberate upon the verdict. I advise you to take a brief respite, and ye shall be summoned once our decision hath been reached."

With that, he led the way, rising from the bench, and the men behind him followed in solemn procession toward the back chamber, leaving the courtroom momentarily hushed and expectant.

The crowd began to discuss and talk about what they think will happen. As half walked out to stretch their legs and smoke outside. This was a moment that they would never have seen in their lives. A woman wanting to be free from her husband despite his behavior.

What will this mean for the men of their generation and the next one? There is so much to consider and the court had to make the right decision not only for them but the people.

Chapter X

I am no longer accepting the things I cannot change.

There were so many emotions in the air and yet only fifteen minutes have passed. It felt as though an hour had passed instead. An hour felt like three. No one knew how this was going to end and gave people different emotions,like stress. There was more smoking going on than normal. When a person looked around there before.

David Colon and the lawyer just chatted together as though they were at a bar having no care in the world. They had no fear because they felt they had the most back up and they did their job making sure the courts knew what was at risk if they chose Ana.

Ana was near her lawyer and her best friend. They were sitting on a bench just hoping that they would see the truth and grant her the one

thing she was hoping for. Finally everyone heard the court officer call everyone in.

"A judgment hath been reached. Pray return unto the court." Everyone started moving. Cigarettes were being turned off and stepped on as they walked to the courtroom. No one had any clue what will happen but they know in a few words it will be over. As people walked in and began to sit it became a bit more quieter. I think the nervousness started to hit some of the people.

As the court clerks started to walk in and the judge was right behind them. They were all about to sit when they heard a noise.

They heard yelling. The judge looked at the Court officer and said. "Find out what is going on outside." The office nodded and went outside. He went to see what the fuss was about.

He walked outside and there were over 80 women, maybe more right in front of the court building. The officer asked 'What dost thou here? Knowest thou not that a case is even now in progress? The Judge is displeased. I counsel thee to return unto thy home, or whencesoever thou camest, that we may proceed with our duty.'" He felt as if he did justice as they all looked at him and two people yelled. *"I am no longer accepting the things I*

cannot change. This shall change or we will make it!"

All the ladies shouted after "*This shall change or we will make it!"*

The court officer called in his men to help him as he went back to the judge to let him know what was going on. He came up to the judge as whispered in his ear what was going on and how the woman refused to go back home.

He also whispered "Should we take them all in your honor? I doubt we have space but we can try." The judge went to the window and looked outside. All the women were still chatting and they were fighting against other officers. He looked back and said to the officer."Nay, I shall see to this matter myself. We must proceed."

The officer nodded and went into front of the court and said out loud for the court's people to hear yet the loudness of the woman chatting was still a bit loud.

"We shall proceed. Pray, compose yourselves and return unto your seats." All of the people went back to their seats and looked at the front of the court.

Not sure what to expect they all looked to the judge waiting for what will happen next.

"I am well aware that there are matters afoot at this present hour which lie beyond our governance. I know also that passions run high, and that this case draweth near its end. Yet I require thee now to compose thyself, and not suffer what passeth beyond these walls to sway thy conduct within this court.

Therefore, for the remainder of this proceeding, ye shall keep your seats. I thank you. Let us proceed." He sat down as everyone just stood quiet still.

The court officer says "Let the Plaintiff and the Defendant now rise." They rose and so did their lawyers.

"I, together with the officers of this court, did not arrive at this judgment lightly. It hath consumed more days than many of our cases taken together. That which is sought this day is no common practice in this land. We have heard both sides of the matter in full, and likewise the testimonies of their witnesses."

"This day, whatever course we take shall touch us all, and this judgment shall stand as final, though some may hold otherwise. Marriage is a hard estate, and some unions are meant to

be striven for, for we are bound by the vow of better or worse—and most often, so it proveth.”

“This case hath led us unto the worse. When we stand at such a fork in the road, which path are we to choose?”

As the Judge spoke, a great hush fell upon the space without the court. Perchance the officers had brought the crowd to order, so thought the Judge—or perchance they stood silent, eager to hear the judgment to be pronounced.

It fell quiet all around the court building in and out. No one had any clue still what he would choose.They did not know what to feel. Will they be angry or will they be happy? The judge continued talking.

"Upon the proofs laid before us, and having duly hearkened unto the closing arguments,we have resolved this day in open court that this province lieth within the New England quarter of the Northeastern Colonies.

Boston is likewise known as the chief and greatest town of the Province of Massachusetts.Therefore, whatever judgment we render this day shall bear consequence upon all of Massachusetts. Our verdict is thus…" The judge just looked at both sides and wondered if he was making the right decision.

In his mind there was no right decision but in his heart he knew what he had to do. Ana's heart was beating fast and her palms were sweaty.

David just stood as calm as day and smiled at his lawyer. The courts will be stupid go against him for he is one of well known men and what he was apple of on this land.

The judge began to talk again after two seconds yet it felt like ten minutes to everyone.

"Beyond all reasonable doubt, we do grant unto the Plaintiff the separation she hath rightfully earned. In truth, the two stand not lawfully wed, for the man was already bound in marriage to his first wife, unto whom we likewise grant a decree of separation."

The crowd went crazy, the men yelled and argued with and the woman screamed for happiness. Ana cried and so did Charlotte as they hugged and thanked the lawyer.

Ana and Charlotte walked hand in hand out the courtroom smiling. Outside of the courtroom David was there so angry and then yelled out to Ana.

"Thou art no wife of mine henceforth; thou hast no claim to remain within my house, nor shall my servants any longer attend thee or so much as acknowledge thy presence."David felt like he had the upper hand.

Ana then responded "David, thy servants already render me no service." Then Charlotte also responded "As for lodging, she may now dwell where she doth choose. Until such time, she may abide with me—if that be agreeable unto thee, Ana?"

Ana smiled back at Charlotte and said. "Why, I thank thee kindly; such generosity is most welcome."

David's response was. "She doth not even dwell within this land. She hath no voice nor claim herein."
Ana looked at him and said.
"Well then, I suppose I won't dwell in this land either." Both of the ladies laughed and began to walk away from him leaving him to his selfish ways.

David just looked stuck and out of words as he watched the two wives he had now not his wives at all, just walking away from him like it didn't mean anything to them.

As the ladies walked out the building they were surprised to see the amount of women in front of the building cheering them on.

There were more women who showed up after the first time the court officer came out and went back in.

They waved and were hugged by so many people. Ana asked one of the ladies congratulating them.

"How came these ladies by such knowledge of our plight? We are but a pair of nobodies—no queens, nor persons of any great estate."

A voice came out from the crowd. A woman walked past the few ladies in front and said. "You are indeed of worth. You have contended for our liberty against thy abuser and the cruel man he proved to be. If thou hast won a separation, then any woman who suffereth such wrongs may now dare to hope she too hath a chance." It was Eric's wife Allice from the court clerks on the case.

Behind her from the crowd came out the house maid with Ana's children.They screamed "Mom" they ran and hugged her so tight. Tears ran a bit down her face to see them after everything she has been through.

"What befell thee, and by what means didst thou convey the children forth from the house without David's leave? I would not want any harm to come unto thee." Ana seemed concerned and knew what David is capable of.

"Master David hath declared that, shouldst thou prevail, he would have no further need of them, for he desireth no dealings with thy offspring, whom he did most cruelly call 'spawns.' Madam, if it pleases thee, I would humbly ask leave to join thee and to continue in the rearing and care of the children." She looked down on the ground while saying this because she did not know the outcome after asking.

"Of course you may join us but my funds are low and I know you have a family." Ana knew saying this that it was one fight does not mean there is not a battle ahead.

Charlotte stated after that "Do not worry neither you or.." She did not know the maiden's name. Waiting for her to answer.

She felt that what they were doing needed to be told and she talked to a few women who spoke to other women who spoke to many others. The rumors not only went through the land but form many others across the land as well.
Women who have traveled to see for themselves the woman fighting for the women who have been hurt, abused mentally or physically and those who decided to go elsewhere then stay in their own marriage.

From that day on Ana and Charlotte became the voices for the woman who wants out of their marriage.

They gave advice around the lands and gave voice to the woman letting them know they are not alone.

It was said that David Colon left the land after people started turning their back on him. They did not want to be acquainted with a man with his reputation. Even Jacob cut ties after that day in the court to protect his company. David was not to be seen again.

The two women still live with each other, also bringing other women into their home who need a safe place to be. As for Eric and Alice they had two more children.

Eric became a judge after seeing how the world can be swayed in so many ways and he wanted to do good in the world.

Yet They have three children now Alice still helps Ana and Charlotte from her land becoming a spokesman for the battered woman and made an only woman club called "Woman Rise up."

Ana's daughter joined her mother in the crusade of justice and her son married a beautiful well-mannered woman with 3 children and treated his wife like a queen.

The End

In the first record of a legal divorce in the American colonies, Anne Clarke of the Massachusetts Bay Colony is granted a divorce from her absent and adulterous husband, Denis Clarke, by the Quarter Court of Boston, Massachusetts.

Polygamy as a crime originated in the common law, and it is now outlawed in every state. In the United States,polygamy was declared unlawful **through the passing of Edmunds Anti-Polygamy Act of 1882**.

End my Marriage

Other stories written by
Vanessa Concepcion-Limage
The Ride home
Fairy Riley Rose
My heart chooses for me

To all my readers, thank you for all your support!

Find me on IG, Facebook, and Tiktok

For more of my work.

(Vanessaawriter@gmail.com)